MYSTERY ON SAFARI

MYSTERY ON SAFARI

Betty Cavanna

Illustrations by Joseph Cellini

William Morrow & Company   New York

BY THE SAME AUTHOR

Published by William Morrow and Company

ACCENT ON APRIL • ALMOST LIKE SISTERS
ANGEL ON SKIS • THE BOY NEXT DOOR
A BREATH OF FRESH AIR • THE COUNTRY COUSIN
FANCY FREE • JENNY KIMURA
MYSTERY AT LOVE'S CREEK • MYSTERY IN MARRAKECH
PASSPORT TO ROMANCE • THE SCARLET SAIL
SPICE ISLAND MYSTERY • STARS IN HER EYES
A TIME FOR TENDERNESS

Published by The Westminster Press

THE BLACK SPANIEL MYSTERY • A GIRL CAN DREAM
GOING ON SIXTEEN • LASSO YOUR HEART
LOVE, LAURIE • PAINTBOX SUMMER
PUPPY STAKES • 6 ON EASY STREET
SPRING COMES RIDING • SPURS FOR SUZANNA
A TOUCH OF MAGIC • TWO'S COMPANY

1

"She'll never let you," Kim explained firmly. "You don't know Miss Peabody."

"Pooh," replied her grandmother.

Kim stifled a sigh and lifted the long hair from her neck with a gnawed yellow pencil, then lay flat on her bed with the telephone balanced on her stomach. "Look, Grandy, she's really strict."

"I've never known a headmistress yet I couldn't get round," said Mrs. Gardiner across the miles that separated New York from the Boston suburbs. Kim could almost see the grin starting at the corners of her grandmother's mouth and the light of conquest in her eyes. Carefully plucked brows, badge of another generation, would be quizzically raised. "Even when I was in school."

Kim was too polite to remind her grandmother that

she hadn't been in school for forty years. Instead, she murmured, "I have no luck with Peebee at all. Could be there's a generation gap."

"Naturally," chortled Mrs. Gardiner. "But Miss Peabody is forward-looking educationally, isn't she, dear?"

"I suppose so, Grandy, but that doesn't mean she'll let you haul me out of school at midterm on the pretext of—well, on any pretext at all."

"East Africa, Kim, darling, is not a pretext. It's a continent. At least I think it's a continent," Mrs. Gardiner amended. "I flunked third-grade geography. In any event, it's full of emerging nations and wild animals, which can be very educational. Very!" She spoke with a rising inflection, an undaunted purposefulness.

"Give up, Grandy. She won't buy it."

"Buy what?" asked Kim's roommate from across the room, where she was leafing through an algebra book morosely.

Kim covered the receiver with the palm of her free hand. "My swinging grandmother thinks she can talk Peebee into letting me off for an extra two weeks at midterm. Fat chance!"

Meanwhile, Mrs. Gardiner was inquiring from her end of the line, "Want to bet?"

Kim considered the remnants of her monthly allowance. "All I've got is a dollar."

"A dollar it is!" cried her grandmother blithely. "Tell me, is Miss Peabody more amenable before or after dinner? In other words, should I phone her now or later? Oh, Kim, sweetie, we will have fun!"

Groaning, Kim put the receiver back in its cradle and flung her pencil across the room. "Grandy's mad." She sighed. "Stark, raving, utterly. Africa yet. What will she think of next?"

Kim's roommate closed her algebra book, gazed dreamily at the trampled snow outside the dormitory window, and said, shivering slightly, "It would be warm in Africa." Raised in Texas, Phillipa never could accustom herself to New England winters and refused to learn to ski.

Kim reached for a Kleenex, blew her nose, then returned to nibbling a fresh pencil. "It doesn't mean a thing to Grandy that exams start tomorrow," she grumbled. "I'll bet when she was our age she never cracked a book."

Amusement flickered in Phillipa's dark eyes. "Maybe it runs in the family."

Kim wrinkled her nose and wound her straight red hair in a Psyche knot on top of her head, anchoring it with the new pencil. "Oh, shut up," she suggested amiably, then turned over on her stomach and propped her history notebook against a pile of pillows at the head of the bed.

"I'll see Catherine Kimberly next."

The voice over the intercom was crisp and business-like and at the same time cultivated, the sort of voice that should belong to a headmistress, but seldom does.

Kim instinctively straightened her skirt as she rose from a chair in the anteroom and followed the secretary's nod toward the office door. "Good morning, Miss Peabody," Kim said, as she stepped inside.

"You may close the door, Catherine."

Kim did as she was told, mentally sizing up the attitude of the tall woman behind the desk. Straight back, gray eyes uncompromisingly direct, the fingertips of one hand pressed pedantically against the fingertips of the other.

"Sit down," Miss Peabody invited. "I suppose you know that your grandmother has been in touch with me."

Kim couldn't stifle a groan. "I told her she was wasting her time," she said apologetically, "but Grandy is very headstrong. I'm sorry, Miss Peabody."

The headmistress frowned. "Headstrong? That's scarcely an adjective that should be applied by one so young to one so full of years. Imperious, perhaps, but not headstrong."

Kim accepted the rebuke and waited. She could have wished her grandmother safely tucked away on some remote Caribbean island, out of reach of a telephone.

"It seems she wishes you to accompany her on an African safari. Are you aware of this?"

Nodding miserably, Kim said, "I told her—" but Miss Peabody interrupted.

"Apparently she is leaving almost immediately."

"Grandy always does things almost immediately," Kim replied.

"To be gone three weeks."

Kim nodded again and blurted, "I told her I couldn't go."

"Your exams are finished when?"

"Thursday," said Kim.

"So that in the normal course of events you would have ten days between terms." Miss Peabody drew a desk calendar toward her. "In effect, she was suggesting that you be released from classes here for an additional eleven days. How have your grades been this past semester, Catherine?"

A flicker of hope was quickly extinguished. "Average," replied Kim honestly.

"Perhaps she is right, that what you lack is a sense of commitment," suggested Miss Peabody while Kim fumed. Grandy had no right to knife her in the back in an attempt to gain her own ends!

"You come from an above-average family," Miss Peabody continued. "Your father an engineer, your mother a writer, your grandmother—like Rachel Carson—an ardent conservationist."

"Grandy started as a bird watcher, way back when," Kim explained. "Now she's president of some sort of wildlife rescue league."

"She has enormous vitality," Miss Peabody said.

Kim couldn't dispute that.

"Although it may be quite unorthodox, as your grandmother pointed out, I do feel that three weeks

9

in Kenya and Tanzania, in the emerging nations of East Africa, might help to focus your attention on something besides skiing weekends. I suppose you would have no objection to doing a term paper for your social studies course on some aspect of your experiences?"

Kim's lower lip dropped until she felt that it was hanging on her chin. "You don't—you can't—"

Miss Peabody nodded. "I have your parents' permission to excuse you from classes for eleven days at the beginning of the new term. Your grandmother has agreed to be responsible for your introduction into a civilization about which too little is known. Be alert. Do your best. I wish you every success, Catherine." Miss Peabody arose, angular and statuesque at the same time, the desk top dwarfed beneath her unusual height. "And now good day."

Nairobi!

From the air the capital of Kenya tilted dangerously as the great plane swung in for a landing. From the ground the city looked like a prairie town in the midst of a building boom. At its elevation of five thousand feet the climate was gracious—much cooler than Kim had anticipated—and the people on the streets looked vigorous.

In a Japanese-made taxi she and her grandmother were whisked from the airport to the Norfolk Hotel, an old-fashioned, rambling conglomeration of buildings encircling a huge interior court where Land Rovers nudged safari buses and private cars. The black reservations clerk spoke with a British accent and handed Mrs. Gardiner a sheaf of messages from Colonel Albert Abercrombie, who had arranged her itinerary. The trip finally began to come into focus, as dates from the typed sheets became real and imminent. The names, however, were strange and impossible for Kim to remember: Ngorongoro, Serengeti, Mara Masai, Tsavo. Only Mombasa, a city vaguely located in her mind somewhere on the Indian Ocean, rang a bell.

Almost at once it was time for lunch, served in a dim, high-ceilinged dining room with plain walls, thin curtains, and an air of bygone British colonialism. The waiters wore white *jellabas,* long, hooded robes reaching to their ankles, and some of them took time to smile at the pretty American girl and bow to the brisk, slight woman who accompanied her.

"Iced tea," said Grandy as soon as she was seated. "I'd dearly love some iced tea."

It took twenty-five minutes, but eventually iced tea appeared in a huge pitcher. Liberally spiked with lemon and orange slices, maraschino cherries and sugar, it was a surprising concoction. Grandy took one sip and murmured, "Ugh," but Kim dutifully drank two glassfuls so that she wouldn't offend the waiter.

"I knew you'd be a comfort," Grandy remarked appreciatively.

11

After lunch the time lag became insupportable, and Kim almost fell asleep on her way back across the courtyard, where even the birds in cages scattered through the parking area were drowsy and still. In the bedroom she kicked off her shoes and collapsed, to awaken at dusk, still groggy from the aftereffects of the long flight.

Behind a closed door she could hear her grandmother splashing in the bathtub, humming tunelessly but energetically to herself. Kim stretched, yawned, and called, "Hi, Grandy. It must be evening. How long did I sleep?"

"Four hours," replied Mrs. Gardiner promptly. "You'd better wake up and get dressed, dear. We're due at the Abercrombies' at seven, to meet our professional hunter, Peter Somebody. Doesn't it sound exciting? I can hardly believe we're here!"

Kim yawned again, compulsively, then murmured a few heartfelt syllables of agreement. She was actually quite disoriented, having finished her exams, packed, joined her grandmother at Kennedy Airport, and boarded the Pan Am jet to Kenya in a flurry succeeded by a prolonged daze. That she could have left New York Thursday and it was now only Friday seemed impossible!

A car with a neat black driver was waiting on the cobbled slope leading from the hotel lobby to an avenue bordered by brilliant beds of clipped bougainvillea. Contemporary buildings belonging to the University of Nairobi faced one another along the road, but they were deserted by this time of the evening. So were many of the back streets through which the driver angled, taking a shortcut to a hilly suburban area of green lawns and flower-trellised houses.

He pulled up in a graveled drive, already occupied by several other cars, and introduced Mrs. Gardiner to her host, Colonel Abercrombie, a tall, erect man with a military mustache and an enthusiastic handshake. The colonel led Kim and her grandmother through a big, comfortable living room to a verandah at the rear of the house, and in turn introduced them to his attractive wife, a visiting friend from England, and several other guests, coming finally to Peter Kent.

Sandy-haired, loose-limbed, and sun-tanned, the professional hunter was a man in his early thirties, with a rather diffident manner belied by the most direct blue eyes Kim had ever seen. When he took her hand, he shook it unemphatically, but his gaze was probing. She felt like a butterfly pinned to a piece of cardboard. What sort of person are you? he seemed to be asking. Long red hair, brown eyes, creamy skin, a healthy American feminine figure with the usual long legs and narrow feet, but what sort of person are you?

To her grandmother he seemed to relate more readily, accepting her as an interested and enthusiastic person, traveled but unsophisticated. He seemed to enjoy her quick speech, her ready laughter, and her easy manner. "I had expected you to be much older,"

13

he told her, making the remark a compliment at which Mrs. Gardiner preened.

"Wait until I've jounced along in a Land Rover for a few days!" she warned. "I expect to age rapidly over here."

Peter laughed. "You get used to it," he promised. "You learn to ride the springs of a Land Rover the way your Western cowboys ride a bronco, high in the stirrups and coming down easy. It's the dust you'll mind."

"Dust?"

"There aren't many paved roads in Kenya," Peter reminded her, "aside from the main highways." He glanced at Mrs. Gardiner's silk cocktail dress. "You'll need comfortable, washable clothes."

Kim mentally reappraised her own wardrobe. "I've got only one pair of slacks," she said.

"We can shop tomorrow," her grandmother promised quickly. "I understand we have a day in Nairobi before we start off."

Peter nodded. "Until late afternoon, when we should do a game run in Nairobi National Park. It's only ten minutes from the city, and it's a good introduction to the animals you're going to see."

Mrs. Abercrombie moved up and touched Kim's elbow lightly. "Come meet some of our other guests while your grandmother talks business with Peter," she proposed, and introduced Kim to a stout, middle-aged couple who spoke English with a heavy German

14

accent. They had already been off on safari in Uganda and were planning to continue on to Tanzania. Kim gathered that everything had been, and doubtless would continue to be, *wundershön.*

She spent a polite five minutes in their company, then seized the opportunity to move on across the terrace toward the rose beds bordering the lawn. Never had she seen blossoms of such fantastic size and color. One variety in particular attracted her attention, a magnificent long-stemmed flower with flame-colored petals and a yellow heart. She bent to sniff its fragrance as a voice behind her asked, "You're interested in gardening?"

Kim turned and pushed back the hair which had fallen forward over her face. "Not really," she said to a tall, pallid boy whose features, although still adolescent, were so like Colonel Abercrombie's there could be no question of his parentage. "I was just admiring the size and the color. We have nothing to equal them at home."

"You must be Catherine Kimberly," the boy decided. "That's rather a famous name in Africa."

"Kimberly? Why?"

"The diamond mines, of course."

Kim flushed. "Of course. How stupid of me." Then she added with a grin, "No connection, naturally."

"I'm Neil Abercrombie," her companion said without smiling. "I came in rather late, so we haven't been properly introduced."

To Kim, Neil sounded stuffy, almost patronizing, with his clipped, upper-class accent, which she associated with British motion pictures. Nevertheless, she felt obliged to make conversation. "Do you go to school in England?" she asked.

"Not any longer," Neil replied. "I finished at Harrow last spring. I'd planned to enter the university here, but then I came down with mono, so I've just been lying around recuperating for the past few months."

"Oh." That must explain his pallor, Kim thought, but even if he were as tanned as Peter Kent, she doubted that she'd find him attractive. Something about his manner rubbed her the wrong way.

"Of course I've been able to read a lot, but it's getting to be a bore," Neil admitted. He stifled a yawn, as though he found the conversation slightly boring as well.

"Perhaps you'd like to meet my grandmother," Kim suggested wickedly. She started back toward the terrace.

Neil stopped her by saying, "I've just been talking to Mrs. Gardiner—a charming person!—and we share an interest in conservation. So rare in Americans."

"Why is it rare?" Kim sounded rather testy.

Instead of replying, Neil said, "Forgive me. I didn't mean to be critical. It's just that you have so little opportunity to assess the importance of preserving the big game."

"We have some fairly big game in America," Kim said defensively. "Deer. Buffalo."

"You *had* buffalo, or bison, rather. Now they're almost extinct."

Kim wasn't sure enough of the facts to disagree, nor was she interested in pursuing an argument concerning a subject on which Grandy was her only source of information. "I'm afraid you're talking to the wrong person," she said rudely. "I don't know a thing about conservation and I couldn't care less."

Neil countered with another question. "What *is* your thing?"

"Thing?" Kim stalled, then shrugged. "I'm still in school."

"Of course. But what are you interested in—really?"

Momentarily at a loss for a reply, Kim told the truth. "Skiing."

"Oh, yes. Of course. But I mean what do you get *excited* about?"

Kim shrugged again. "Not much."

"Too bad," Neil said, and walked away as though the conversation, prolonged by his curiosity, had finally and irrevocably come to an end.

2

Kim wondered, the next morning, why she had found Neil Abercrombie so irritating. Fleetingly, she was ashamed of her unnecessary rudeness but realized that such misconduct need cause her no great concern, really, since it was most unlikely that she would ever see the young man again.

After breakfasting late on their own small balcony, Kim and her grandmother started off to explore the city and go shopping for safari clothes. The day was cool and breezy, the sun warm, the air sparkling, and a long night's sleep had restored Kim's vitality and good disposition. She felt so full of energy that she almost skipped down the street.

Nairobi was bustling this morning. The pavements were crowded with a stream of fascinating people—Indian women in saris, Sikhs in turbans, Pakistani girls wearing tight tunics and satin trousers, African businessmen in Western dress, and occasional white tourists. Taxis raced along like small, fat beetles, lorries and buses groaned past, and everywhere there was the noise and purposeful confusion of construction. Nairobi, a pioneer town of one street in 1902, now housed four hundred thousand people. The young capital of Kenya was building upward, and building fast.

Unexpected contrasts were everywhere. Mohammedan mosques huddled under bulbous towers next to high-rise contemporary buildings. A cylindrical hotel stretched skyward like a giant silo. A curio shop selling primitive masks and animal skins adjoined a window filled with imported hair sprays, sun cream, and cosmetics.

Buyers were plentiful, and the store on Kenyatta Avenue, to which Mrs. Gardiner had been directed for safari clothes, was doing a brisk business. There were departments for both men and women, and every clerk was busy, so while her grandmother sat in the shoe section waiting to be fitted with desert boots, Kim wandered about.

Long wooden counters were piled with an assortment of merchandise, green- or khaki-colored shirts and slacks, culottes, skirts, bush jackets, and sweaters. A practiced eye could see at a glance that the quality was good, the clothing well made, and the prices half what they would have been in the United States. In a corner before a pier mirror two men in tropical-weight suits were trying on hats, searching for the right head sizes and, meanwhile, conducting an animated conversation in a foreign language. Kim's attention was caught because, for some strange reason, the dialogue seemed to have nothing to do with their actions. Certainly no article of clothing—and most certainly not the choice of a khaki bush hat!—could elicit the violent whispering, the arm waving and argument that were taking place.

She studied the two men more closely. One was obviously an Indian, slight and swarthy, who looked like any of a hundred Nairobi shopkeepers along these streets. The other she couldn't place, so far as nationality was concerned. He could have been East European. Hair trimmed close to his head above a short neck, recently sunburned, small eyes set unfortunately close together, and a wart on the left side of a thick nose added up to a thoroughly unpleasant physiognomy.

Kim moved closer and started to try on hats herself, since Peter Kent had warned her that she must guard against exposure in the bush. Men's and women's models were mixed together, but the masculine hats appealed to her more than the feminine, and she especially favored the wide-brimmed copies of the headgear worn by Australian soldiers.

The two men glanced briefly in her direction, but without any show of interest. Their argument continued, the whispers changing to a sibilant hissing, which would have seemed amusing to Kim had it not also sounded rather threatening. What could they be talking about?

Her curiosity aroused, she started to move closer when a door on the far side of the shop opened, and a broad-shouldered, stocky man entered. He had short, very curly fair hair and his skin was leathery and tanned from years of outdoor living. Dressed in old, well-laundered shorts and a belted jacket, he had an air of authority about him, and he went directly to a man working at a desk at the rear of the store and spoke in a deep, unusually resonant voice.

"Is my order ready, I wonder? John Sanderson is the name."

Kim was watching him in the mirror as he asked the question, and for a moment she forgot the nearby presence of the pair of argumentative men. When she next glanced in their direction, she was astonished to see that they had abandoned both their controversy and the hats, and were stealing out of the side door as though they were being pursued.

Like actors in a television suspense series, they seemed to be stepping high and softly. Kim burst out laughing as she watched them turn down a side street. Then, still smiling, she walked over to consult her grandmother about the hat selection she had made.

"Like it, Grandy?"

"Very dashing. Why are you so amused?"

21

"Just enjoying a little local color," Kim replied. "I'll tell you about it later." But the incident, after all, was so slight that she forgot it as soon as a sales clerk approached and the serious business of buying began.

Laden with their purchases, they stopped for a lemonade at tables set out in the L-shaped entrance area before the New Stanley Hotel, a midtown meeting place for travelers from all over the world. Hawkers of cheap African wood carvings—giraffes, gazelles, lions, and buffaloes—lined the nearby sidewalk and did a spotty trade in their toy-sized wares.

"Junk," was the word with which Grandy dismissed the carvings, but Kim lingered beside the East Indian salesman and was tempted to invest a dollar in one of the little animals. "Mother and Dad sent me a check for spending money, and I want to take something back to my roommate. Don't you think—?"

Grandy shook her head firmly. "You'll find more interesting carving out in the country, I'm quite sure."

Kim glanced back toward the vendor, who was still holding out a small giraffe hopefully, and shook her head. "Why are they always Indians?" she wondered aloud. "The merchants and sales help. Why aren't they Africans?"

With a shrug Grandy said, "It's the same all over the world. In the Fiji Islands, in Tahiti, and even in the Caribbean, a great many Indians keep store. It seems to be their special milieu."

"Ellen Gardiner!"

Grandy glanced up in astonishment to look into the eyes of a plump, gray-haired woman who loomed above the table like a large pink balloon. "Mopsy! Well, this is a surprise! Imagine meeting here, halfway around the world." Stretching out a hand in greeting, she drew the woman down to a chair and introduced Kim, explaining, "Mrs. Collins and I were in the same class in school and we've seen each other occasionally ever since."

Kim found it hard to believe that this matronly woman could be the same age as her trim little grandmother, whose neatly coifed hair was carefully tinted to maintain its original red-gold color, and whose figure was still a size twelve.

Amenities were being exchanged. "You look marvelous, Ellen."

"And so do you."

I hope Grandy has her fingers crossed, Kim thought, because in her opinion Mrs. Collins should have chosen any color for a traveling costume except bright pink.

"Are you going to the game parks or are you just passing through?" asked Mrs. Collins, glancing at the chair stacked with packages.

"We're leaving on safari tomorrow."

"What a coincidence! So are we. I'm here with three friends from home, all widows, and we're starting off first thing in the morning. Are you on a bus tour? We're with Zebra."

Mentally, Kim groaned. She adored her grandmother and found her a delightful traveling companion, but she could imagine nothing more dismal than being trailed through East Africa by Mrs. Collins and her friends, whom she could already envision. While Grandy explained that she and Kim were traveling by Land Rover along with a "nice young man who is a professional hunter," the lemonade arrived.

"What may we order for you, Mopsy?"

"Oh, nothing, thank you. I must be getting along, but perhaps our paths will cross somewhere out in the wilds."

If any woman looked unequipped to go into the wilds, it was Mopsy Collins, Kim thought. She was wearing high-heeled white slippers, a pearl necklace with matching earrings, and the purse she was balancing safely on her lap was a huge affair of white straw decorated with raffia flowers.

"Perhaps." Grandy's light, quick laugh made Kim wonder whether the remark was hopeful or pessimistic. "I understand the wilds have become pretty tame, now that photographic safaris are all the rage and we're required to stay safely inside our cars."

"And a good thing, too." Mrs. Collins gave a slight shiver. "I do hope we're going to enjoy all this. I sometimes think, at our age, it's a little daring, just to be here at all."

Grandy laughed again, and this time there was no mistaking the fact that her amusement held a certain scorn. "Nonsense, Mopsy, derring-do may have entered into safaris in the old days, when travelers went into the highlands on foot, accompanied by a couple of dozen bearers, but now you'll be as safe as though you were in your rocking chair at home."

"Well, I do hope so." Mrs. Collins gave a sigh as she rose to leave. "I must say you sound intrepid, Ellen." Then she turned to Kim. "So very pleasant to have met you, my dear."

After lunch, while her grandmother curled up on her bed with a book by Elspeth Huxley, whose account of her childhood in Africa apparently made fascinating reading, Kim went back downtown to look for a belt to wear with her slacks. She had seen some skin belts that interested her, in particular some made of leopard hide, and she decided to try to find one that could be worn both with dresses and pants.

The walk along Government Road and University Way was pleasant, and at Muindi Mbingu Street she turned toward busy Kenyatta Avenue and the part of town she had visited that morning. Window shopping, she strolled along, completely comfortable among the crowds of genial people, handsome in their rich blackness and their picturesque, bright-colored garments. Already she could separate the simple, primitive villagers, probably in Nairobi for a brief day's excursion, from the tough, humorous, resilient city dwellers who were clothed, almost invariably, in white shirts and dark Western trousers. These people strode along with authority, as though they were strong, vital, and happy in their new nationhood. They smiled at her when she came face-to-face with them, men and women alike, and after a few such encounters Kim realized they were amused and attracted by her long red hair.

In a curio shop with wide doors open to the street all sorts of skin belts were displayed—leopard, zebra, lion, and antelope hides bound in black leather. Kim ventured inside a trifle timidly, but at once found that she was free to wander around and handle the merchandise, which consisted mainly of curios; in addition there were purses and wallets, eyeglass cases and throw rugs, all made of animal skins.

The proprietor, one of the ubiquitous Indians, was occupied at the back of the store with a middle-aged couple who were obviously Americans. The man, a thin, nervous type with a freckled and sunburned bald head, was considering a succession of leopard pelts thrown on the floor in front of him. His wife, wearing dark glasses and an armful of heavy gold bracelets, was standing by with her lips pursed, except when a quoted price elicited squeals of protest.

The furrier, Kim thought, was very patient. "You realize, madam," he said soothingly, "that coats made from pelts of this quality are selling for twenty-four thousand dollars in London. Examine the thickness, if you will." He lifted an edge of the top skin. "Feel!"

The woman bent gingerly and touched the fur with

the tips of her fingers, almost as though she were afraid the creature, whose beautiful small head had been kept intact, would turn and bite. "But I don't want a coat, Willard," she complained to her husband in a petulant voice. "I just want a rug to put in front of the playroom fireplace."

Kim turned away to hide a smile. She glanced again at the woman's profile, the crepey chin, the wrinkles starting around the mouth, the blond-tinted, fluffy hair. If I saw her on Fifth Avenue, she thought, I wouldn't look twice, but here she seems strange and out of place.

The husband was beginning to bargain. "You guarantee it's a genuine Somali leopard?"

"Oh, yes, sir," said the Indian unctuously.

"Maybe we ought to wait until we go to Somaliland, Willard. Maybe the prices there will be lower. What do you think?"

"It's Ethiopia we're going to, not Somalia." Willard took a cigar from his jacket pocket and stripped off its cellophane covering. Then he placed it between his teeth without lighting it and said, bluntly, "I understand top quality pelts are going in Nairobi for five hundred, no more."

The Indian looked horrified. He spread his hands, shrugged, and said to Kim in a raised voice that would be sure to carry, "I'll be with you in a minute, miss." Then he turned back to the American couple and said, very quietly, "I'm afraid you've been misinformed."

Now Kim watched and listened shamelessly. She was in no hurry. Furthermore, the wait, obviously, would be a long one. Willard was just warming up to this game. He was beginning to have fun.

"I'll tell you what. I'll make it six hundred. You pack and ship."

The furrier shook his head gently. "I'm very sorry," he said. "One minute. I will show you another skin within the price range you speak of. Perhaps, since you wish to use it as a rug, it will be quite adequate."

He turned toward a storeroom at the back of the shop, while Willard lit his cigar and said to his wife, "Robbers, all of 'em."

His wife nodded and sighed. "My feet are beginning to hurt, dear. Let's get back to the hotel and take a nap."

She came over and sat on a stool near the counter at which Kim was stationed, casting a faint smile in her direction. The storekeeper, meanwhile, had returned with a smaller, less brilliantly marked pelt.

At this Willard positively sneered. He moved to another part of the store, priced a primitive ebony carving and some small ivory figurines, then came back to the subject of skins, ignoring the fact that Kim was still patiently waiting. "Five-fifty," he barked, "and I'll do the shipping. That's my top price."

The Indian bowed but shook his head. "I am sorry, sir, but I cannot agree," he said politely, and came over to stand behind the counter facing Kim.

"All I want," she said, "is to buy a belt." She was

about to say, "A leopard skin belt," but suddenly she changed her mind. "A plain black leather belt, if you have one," she said instead, while from the corner of her eye she saw Willard stamp angrily out of the store, his wife following, in her tight, patent-leather shoes, several paces behind.

Nairobi National Park was incredibly close to the city. It took Peter Kent only ten minutes to drive the two and a half miles to the main gate. Mrs. Gardiner rode in front, Kim in back, jouncing along on the hard springs of the Land Rover's seat as though she were sitting to the trot of a horse.

The ticket takers and guards wore neat khaki shorts and jackets. One was tall and slender and belonged to the Masai tribe, according to Peter, and the other was short and positively skinny, with pierced earlobes weighted with heavy ornaments that stretched the skin grotesquely, almost to his shoulders. When he smiled at Kim with a grin that displayed many gaps between his teeth, she scarcely could control a shudder. "He's a Kikuyu," Peter said as they drove on.

"I wouldn't want to meet him on a dark night," Kim murmured.

"Oh, he's quite harmless, a very nice fellow, really. He's been a guard here for years." Peter drove slowly through a wooded section, called the Langata corner, and kept peering from one side of the road to the other, alert for game.

"You might call this an animal suburb," he said as

he drove. "There are a few families who live in the park by long-established right, but mainly it's an animal housing development. Look, there's an impala, back under the trees."

Mrs. Gardiner trained her binoculars on the spot Peter indicated. "He must have perfect camouflage."

Then the animal moved, and in a flash disappeared in the undergrowth, but the flash had been sufficient for Kim to glimpse a beautiful brown buck with a white belly and horns shaped like a lyre, graceful as a deer as he leaped out of sight. "Isn't he beautiful!" she breathed.

A few minutes later they came out of the woods and drove along a dirt track through a stretch of grassland that extended to the horizon. Kim found it hard to believe that the city lay just a few miles behind them, because here grazed herds of gazelles and zebras, moving across the savanna as though the clouds of dust raised by tourists' cars concerned them not at all.

"Do they feed these creatures?" Mrs. Gardiner asked.

Peter shook his head. "They live here just as they do in the interior."

"Why don't people ride zebras?" Kim mused. They looked to her like little striped horses, fleet of foot and easy to mount.

"I used to wonder that same thing when I was a boy." Peter turned from the wheel to speak to Kim. "Actually, South Africans broke them to harness and used them with mules to carry the mail coaches, back in the old days. But the zebras quickly sickened and died. They're not very strong, you see."

Always, Kim noticed, Peter spoke of animals gently, almost lovingly. She wondered how it happened that he had become a professional hunter, because surely this entailed killing the wildlife Grandy and a host of others were now so interested in preserving. She must remember to ask him, someday, how he had come to choose this particular career.

But right now her first sight of wild game was more important than putting questions to their guide. In the distance loomed a solitary giraffe, standing twenty feet high against the bright blue sky. Peter stopped the car while they watched him nibble at the leaves of low-growing trees, then move off across the open plain, his long neck bobbing back and forth with every stride. The gazelles reminded Kim of deer, the zebras of small horses, but the giraffe was a completely incredible animal, looking like nothing else on earth. She turned and followed him in fascination through her binoculars until he disappeared from sight.

A Toyota, the Japanese version of a Land Rover, came slowly past, heading back toward the Langata corner, and Peter leaned out to hail the black driver. *"Wapi simba?"* he asked.

After a brief exchange in Swahili, Peter nodded and said thank you in English as he put the car into gear.

Kim's curiosity was aroused. "What were you asking him?"

"Whether he had seen any lions."

"And had he?" Mrs. Gardiner inquired.

Peter nodded. "We'll go take a look at him, if you like."

"Him?" repeated Kim.

Peter nodded, then grinned. "I'm afraid he's not a very exciting specimen, actually. An old male who has left the pride. We'll do better later on."

Still, Kim and her grandmother were both excited at the prospect of seeing their first wild lion. As they drove on, raising a cloud of dust in their wake, they exchanged a smile of anticipation. *"Wapi simba,"* Kim repeated under her breath.

The lion who roared from the motion picture screen to introduce a film. *Simba.* Muted thunder with a rasping edge, the voice of primeval Africa! She felt a thrill of expectation trace its way up her spine as Peter turned off the track and started across country toward a clutch of cars parked near a small grove of trees.

Then disappointment stung her. As the Land Rover edged into the circle of Volkswagen buses, safari cars, and other more conventional vehicles, Kim was torn between disgust and wry amusement. One tired old lion, his ruff scroungy and matted, lay sleeping in the grass. Although he was motionless and almost invisible in the foot-high vegetation, a dozen tourists were taking pictures. Movie cameras buzzed away from the open hatches of the buses, and the shutters of still cameras clicked softly, not disturbing the old fellow in the least.

After a while he rolled over, cocked a sleepy eye at his visitors, and flopped down to face in the opposite direction. "Why, he's as tame as a kitten," Kim fumed.

"Don't you believe it!" Peter warned. "But it is pretty funny. In the old days when Frank Buck and that crowd were mucking about in the veldt, the white hunters used to look for lions at the tail end of the huge zebra migrations. A pride would follow along to pounce on cripples who couldn't keep up with the herd. But now that we have game parks and photographic safaris instead of trophy hunting, we look for exhaust fumes on the horizon. In some ways it's a pity, but, on the other hand, the more tourists we attract, the more chance there is that the wild animals will be preserved."

"Have you done much actual hunting, Peter?" Grandy asked Kim's unspoken question.

"Enough," Peter replied. "I don't like killing, but some parts of the country occasionally become overpopulated with game, and professional hunters are hired to go in and restore the balance of nature." His lips curved in a wry smile. "That took care of itself in the old days, but progress has its problems."

Kim was scarcely listening. The circle of cars and the ruddy-faced German in the adjacent bus, adjusting his telephoto attachment, made her feel cheated. If this is what Grandy had brought her all this distance to see, she might as well have stayed home! One measly old lion breathing in carbon monoxide by the lungful. Kim, raised on television documentaries and Hemingway descriptions, muttered, "Savage splendor, my eye."

In fact, her disappointment would have been insurmountable had she not sustained a subsequent, and more lasting, shock. As Peter drove back through the twilight toward the twinkling lights of Nairobi, he turned, conversationally, to Mrs. Gardiner. "By the way," he said, "Colonel Abercrombie wonders if I may have permission to bring his son, Neil, along on our safari. He's recuperating from mononucleosis, as I think you know, and the colonel feels that a couple of weeks in the open would do him good."

Kim, in the back seat, closed her eyes and waited for her grandmother's reply. "For Pete's sake, Grandy," she silently begged, "stand up for your rights. Say no!"

3

Skirting lorries and mammy wagons, cows, children, and countless women with babies on their backs and baskets on their heads, the Land Rover rattled past the Aberdare Mountains toward Nyeri and the Outspan Hotel.

In the rear rode the luggage and picnic equipment, on the second seat Kim and her grandmother jounced along, and in front, next to the driver, sat Neil Abercrombie, looking appropriately pale and sickly compared to Peter Kent.

"Don't be silly, darling," Grandy had said, brushing off with a wave of her hand Kim's objection to Neil's inclusion on the safari. "What could I say, except yes? After all, there *is* an extra seat in the car, and I thought you'd enjoy some young companionship."

Ebulliently friendly, her grandmother would never

understand that certain boys would have been welcome, but others—well! Kim recognized, however, that the decision was not to be countermanded. Whether she liked Neil or not, she was stuck with him for a fortnight.

Right now he was explaining to Grandy why it was necessary to stop at the Outspan on the way to Treetops, the famous hotel built on high stilts among several huge old trees. "Both places are run by the same company, you see. After lunch you'll make the final leg of the trip in Outspan buses. We aren't allowed to take our own car in."

"Why not?" Mrs. Gardiner asked.

"One of the rules," Neil replied. "Like being allowed to stay only one night, because of the enormous demand. Last year they booked more than ten thousand people, didn't they, Peter?"

Peter Kent nodded. "Some of our clients think Treetops is a tourist trap," he admitted candidly, "but no safari is complete without a stop there. The view of the water hole and the salt lick is spectacular, and you're absolutely sure to see animals."

"The present hotel isn't the original one, you know." Neil turned in his seat and spoke to Mrs. Gardiner exclusively, since Kim was only half listening. "That was literally in a tree. The present Queen of England was staying there in 1952 the night her father died, so there's a saying that Elizabeth went up a tree a princess and came down a queen."

"What happened to the old hotel?" Kim aroused herself to ask.

"It was burned down during the Mau Mau uprising. When the owners rebuilt they expanded, and now it's really very comfortable."

Only after lunch did Kim and her grandmother realize that Peter and Neil would stay behind at the Outspan. "Guides and hunters can't be accommodated," Peter explained. "There just isn't room."

Eventually, therefore, Kim found herself being shepherded on foot from the bus to the hotel by another hunter, a towering, beak-nosed Britisher in khaki shorts and high socks with a rifle slung over his shoulder. His name was Colonel Hayes-Newington, and Kim learned that he had been an officer in the Indian Army before World War II, which to her seemed an incredibly long time ago. Then he had commanded a brigade in Burma and later, during the Mau Mau uprising, served as a staff officer in the Kenya police.

In a grave, courteous manner he warned the busload of tourists that wild animals might be about, and that in case one appeared there were "hides," reedscreened enclosures, on either side of the path where people could seek shelter. "Once in a while we get a stray rhino or buffalo, or occasionally an elephant," he said. "When you get up in the trees the only menace is the baboons. They have a nasty habit of grabbing your film and stringing it out. In fact, they'll make off with anything they can find, so if you're away from your room keep the windows locked and the zippers on your luggage closed, if you don't want to lose your possessions."

The short walk to the hotel was so uneventful that Kim felt that the climate of danger was being created deliberately. From the rooftop, half concealed among leafy branches, another gun-bearing guard looked down, but not a single wild animal—not even a chipmunk—could be seen.

Having been maneuvered past all possible attack, the tourists began climbing outside stairs to a three-deck, wooden structure with narrow hallways lined with doors opening into small, twin-cotted rooms. Burdened with binoculars and cameras, Kim and her grandmother continued bravely upward, and found themselves on a flat rooftop surrounded by a sturdy railing and furnished with chairs, a big tea table, and a dozen eager baboons.

Below lay the main attraction—the reason for Treetops' existence—a drinking pond guaranteed to entice animals from miles around to its waters. Even now, in midafternoon, a rhinoceros could be spotted in the distance, approaching with dignity through trees and tall grass toward the far bank. A stray bushbuck came from the opposite direction, trailed by a small, ugly animal holding its tail straight up in the air.

Kim focused her glasses. "What's that, Grandy?" she asked before she realized that her grandmother had moved away to get a better view of the rhino.

"A warthog, my dear. A wild pig, actually. He's

named for the warts on the sides of his face, which you can probably see through those glasses." The answer came from Colonel Hayes-Newington, who was apparently host as well as hunter. He smiled down at Kim in a kindly fashion when she lowered her binoculars and said, "The viewing is usually slow until dusk, but we'll be serving tea up here shortly." Smiling, he added, "Tea for you people and toast for the baboons."

Tea for the tourists included hot buttered scones, various kinds of cake, and succulent rounds of fresh pineapple served on the tines of forks. Afterward the baboons were fed; their numbers had increased markedly as the time for the regular afternoon treat drew near.

They raced along the railings, chasing one another, sometimes in play but at other times in anger, their teeth bared. Thickset, olive-brown and dog-faced, the old males looked treacherous and crafty, but the colonel apparently knew which could be trusted and soon had a gentle animal curled up in one arm, while with his free hand he divided the bread among all who would come close enough to accept it from his fingers. The animals included mothers with babies clinging to their bellies or riding on their backs, youngsters who chattered like teen-agers and snatched impolitely at the proffered food, and an occasional misanthropic individual who sat grumpily on the railing scratching himself and refusing to join the crowd.

"Here, hand this to Nellie. She's a gentle sort." The

colonel offered a piece of toast to Kim and indicated a smallish female. "Don't drop it now. Make her take it from you, the way she does from me."

But Nellie had other ideas. At that very moment she spied a cigar sticking out of the pocket of a plaid jacket. Reaching out, she snatched it deftly and ran away with it, while the owner cried "Hey, you!" ineffectually.

Glancing at the victim, Kim recognized Willard, the American who had been so obnoxious in the Nairobi curio shop. She smiled to herself, rather glad he had lost his cigar. Along with everyone else who had witnessed the incident, she watched in amusement as the baboon began to eat her trophy, cellophane and all. I hope it was an expensive one, she thought.

Although he was standing right beside her, Willard obviously didn't remember Kim. He turned to talk to a tall, handsome man who was fitting a long-focus lens on a Hasselblad.

"That looks like a great camera you have there."

"Many people consider it the best in the world," said the tall man with a trace of Prussian arrogance. He had an erect, almost military bearing, steel-blue eyes, and thinning hair. Except for his noticeable German accent, he could have passed as the twin brother of Prince Philip.

"Do you know our Polaroid?" Willard was asking. "It gives you a colored picture in less than a minute. You can't beat that!"

"But in comparison to the Hasselblad the Land Camera is a toy," said the German with a slight smile. He turned away to focus on a baboon mother and baby.

Willard clung to him like a gnat, however, and a few minutes later Kim heard the pair discussing customs, tariffs, and something called the skin game. "Is there still a black market in leopard hides?" the American asked.

The German shrugged. "So they say."

"I'm looking for a present for the wife, you see, and I was wondering—"

Before Kim could hear anything more, the two men moved off. She followed behind, curious, but midway down the line of chairs her grandmother beckoned. "Look, Kim, look! Coming through the trees over on the right. Buffaloes, dozens of buffaloes!"

Out of the forested hills beyond Treetops and into the reeds bordering the water hole came a stream of massive, charcoal-colored animals with down-sweeping, widely curved horns helmeting their foreheads. They marched along deliberately, spreading out at the water's edge and wading right into the pond to drink. Kim began to count them, and soon the number was more than a hundred. Yet still they came out of the trees, one herd blending with another, stopping to drink or wallow for a while at the water hole, then moving quietly off into the forest on the opposite side.

The baboons disappeared, pounding down the out-

41

side steps of the hotel or sliding down the drainpipes, while Kim, mesmerized by the oncoming herds, continued to count. "Three hundred and two, three, four, five. . . ." The sun was setting, and the evening chill was making her grandmother shiver.

"I'm going down to the room, dear," she said, and pushed back her chair.

"I'll come along." Through her binoculars Kim could see perhaps a hundred more of the ponderous, bovine beasts silhouetted against the light coming through the scattered trees. For the first time she was catching a glimpse of the sheer vastness of Africa. Four hundred uncaged, dangerous animals within a square mile! The sight made her sense a kind of grandeur in this remarkable country for which she had been quite unprepared. "Tourist trap or not, this is marvelous!" she cried.

Nobody changed for dinner, because travelers were limited by strict rule to small overnight bags and the clothes on their backs. By dark the bar was crowded, as were the economy-class seats from retired BOAC planes, which lined the narrow porches facing the water hole.

The night was really chilly. Wrapped in blankets, the hotel guests looked to Kim like patients in a hospital. They talked in whispers, so as not to disturb the animals, and an occasional burst of laughter from the bar made them turn their heads and frown.

Banging on a gong, the colonel announced the evening meal, and Kim and her grandmother slid onto benches at one of the long tables down the center of which ran a toy track. A three-course meal was moving along on small flatcars. From the trolley each guest picked his own bowl of soup and upon finishing exchanged it for a plate bearing sliced beef, potatoes, and vegetables, all of which had been prepared at the Outspan and brought up here by truck.

Kim was seated next to a congenial girl from South Africa whose father was a university professor. Here on a short holiday, she had been to a number of the game parks and was leaving the next day for home.

"It's been a super trip," she said, "and for you this is just the beginning. Wait till you get to the Ngorongoro Crater and the Serengeti. It's like stepping back to the beginning of time."

The unfamiliar names meant little or nothing to Kim, but she nodded in anticipation. This afternoon she had caught a glimpse of what might lie ahead.

There was no question of going to bed. Spotlights had been trained on the salt lick and the water hole, where the show was likely to continue until dawn. Buffaloes were still shoving and pushing each other at the water's edge, and two rhinos were facing each other menacingly on the hard, bare ground close to the lodge.

Kim and her grandmother watched from a vantage

point behind a big glass window, as the pair alternately licked salt and raised their heads to snort loudly. With their massive front horns and ungainly bulk, they looked positively prehistoric.

"They can't see very well." Grandy chuckled. "Look at those tiny eyes! Watch the fellow on the left. Each eye gives him a different picture to look at, and each is pretty fuzzy. He can't even see his opponent distinctly."

Kim could understand why. When one of the rhinos cocked his head sideways to see around the bulk of his muzzle and his protruding horn, he was tantalized but confused. If he lowered his horn and charged, he would be running blind.

To Kim's surprise, that is just what he did; a ton and a half of bluff, noisy, wasted energy and sheer ineptitude missed the other rhino by several feet. Decelerating to a stop, he snorted indignantly, then turned and peered anxiously back toward his target. The other rhino didn't move, but he pawed the ground angrily. Clued in once more to his enemy's approximate position, the horned fury galloped toward him, missed, and returned to charge again, without success. Kim burst out laughing.

When the rhino encounter began to pall, there were always buffaloes and various kinds of gazelles to look at, but, although expected, not an elephant appeared. "You can't have everything," the colonel told his guests with a rueful grin.

By midnight the viewing chairs were beginning to empty. "Let's give up and go to bed," Grandy suggested.

Kim, who had been yawning for the past half hour, replied, "It's fine with me."

They could barely move in the space between the cots, and their clothes had to be hung against a rough tree trunk on hooks, but at least Kim felt she was really in the Africa she had read about. Impulsively she leaned over and kissed her grandmother good-night. "I can't thank you enough for bringing me along," she said just before she fell asleep.

It was pitch dark outside the bedroom window, which faced the baboon park rather than the water hole, when Kim suddenly awakened to a banging on the door. Bare feet were running along the hallway, and a soft African voice was calling something unintelligible.

"What's he saying?" she asked, sitting up in bed and feeling for the light switch.

"Sounded like *bongo* to me," said Grandy. "Bongo drums? Why bongo drums? Do you suppose there's a native uprising?" She sounded more teasing than serious.

"Let's go see." As she spoke Kim was already struggling into a robe, which she belted around her waist hastily. "Come on!"

Mrs. Gardiner groped sleepily for her bedroom

slippers. "You go on. I may not make it," she said, yawning, but a few minutes later she was peering over Kim's shoulder on a gallery crowded with tourists in every imaginable stage of dress. Not a person was paying the slightest attention to anyone else, because beside the water hole, just a few yards from the lodge, two bull antelopes, completely ignoring both the floodlights and the spectators, were fighting.

"Bongos," said someone softly. "They're extremely shy and very seldom seen."

"They must be fighting over a female," someone else said, "but where is she?"

"Probably back in the bush somewhere," came the answer. Then quiet was followed by a jarring impact as the two animals locked horns.

Neither Kim nor her grandmother spoke. They stood transfixed by the piercing beauty of the bright chestnut bodies marked with vertical stripes so white they might have been painted on the hide. The open horns were spiral, the dancing feet small and neat. As one bongo pulled away, then moved in and tried to gore the other, Kim stifled a gasp.

Somewhere in the hotel a clock struck three. As though on signal the colonel, fully dressed, appeared and walked along behind the watchers, pausing at intervals to tell everyone that not since the night of Queen Elizabeth's visit had an antelope fight been witnessed at Treetops. "And bongos are very rare. Very!" he repeated. "You are most fortunate."

Kim didn't feel fortunate. She felt scared. "But one of them could kill the other one!" she whispered. "Aren't you going to *do* anything to stop the fight?"

The colonel shook his head, although his eyes were gentle and understanding. "We never do anything to disturb the balance of nature," he told her. "The animals live here just as they have for hundreds of thousands of years, killing and being killed, growing up and dying, without any interference from man."

Kim had to accept this explanation, but it didn't make her happy. She stood twisting the belt of her bathrobe anxiously as the bongos clashed again and again. She wanted to scream. She wanted to run away. She wanted to go back to bed and shut her eyes and her ears, but like her grandmother and the others she seemed incapable of movement. The scene had the fascination of a bullfight, dramatic and utterly compelling, even though, as minute followed minute, everyone came to recognize that this was indeed a fight to the death.

When the conquered bongo fell, his side crimson with blood from the slashes of his opponent, the crowd moaned, and Kim hid her face in her hands. Yet when the victorious male bounded off into the forest, she shared his triumph. "I just hope that girl he's been fighting for is worth it!" Grandy sighed.

When another knock sounded on the door, it was daylight, time to get up, make a cursory toilet in the

47

community bathroom, and traverse the two hundred yards back to the buses, which would take everybody down to the Outspan for a big English breakfast. Kim yawned and burrowed under the covers. "Five more minutes," she begged.

She heard her grandmother pull on some clothes, pick up the kit that contained her toothbrush and other necessities, and close the bedroom door behind her. Then she lifted her arms, stretched, and rubbed her eyelids with the knuckles of both hands. From outside the partially opened window she could hear the chattering of the baboons. Sitting up, she drew the curtain aside and looked down at whole families of them, scampering over the hard-packed ground, swinging themselves up to the hotel roof along the railings, even peeking mischievously into the windows of adjacent rooms.

One furry fellow, with a snout almost as long as a collie dog's, craftily pushed against a casement window and reached quickly inside, then cackled in delight as he emerged with a small green booklet instantly recognizable as an American passport. He sat for a moment, riffling the pages, for all the world as though he were reading, then with a bound hit the steps six feet below and made off with his prize.

Kim knew she had to act quickly, and here she was in her pajamas three stories above the ground. She opened her own window as far as she could and leaned out, searching for some sign of human life below. Of course, since it was forbidden to leave the hotel, not a soul was to be seen, but suddenly she thought of the guard stationed on the roof yesterday. By chance he might be on duty again this morning, but how could she reach him?

There was only one way. She screamed at the top of her healthy American lungs, and the result was almost instantaneous. The disheveled heads of several tourists popped from nearby windows, and a moment later a troubled black face peered down from the rooftop railing. Kim pointed to the escaping baboon. "He's got a passport!"

As if by magic a pair of houseboys appeared on the flight of steps nearest the ground. "Passport!" the guard yelled and pointed.

Wild animals apparently held no terror for these lads, because at once the chase was on. The baboon with his trophy had disappeared into the branches of a nearby fig tree, but the minute the boys started in this direction, the thief swung nimbly to the ground and loped off toward the forest.

One boy ran in a wide circle to head the animal off, and the other approached more slowly, holding out a piece of bread. The baboon hesitated, considered the offering with interest, then tucked the passport under his arm and waddled tentatively toward the familiar food.

From above Kim could hear the servant speak to the baboon in Swahili. The intonation was coaxing. "Come on, fellow," he seemed to be saying. "There's a good boy."

This animal, however, was a tease. He sat down on his haunches, removed the passport from his armpit, and again appeared to study its contents, glancing only occasionally toward the proffered bread.

Meanwhile the second houseboy was creeping up from the rear, but he had no chance of getting close enough to capture the booklet. The baboon's hearing was far too acute. He glanced quickly over his shoulder and bared his teeth. Then, with a gesture so fast that Kim could scarcely follow it, he exchanged the passport for the piece of bread.

From the hotel windows came a burst of spontaneous applause. The baboon stood his ground, as though prepared to take a bow, and the two boys ran swiftly back to the hotel. Kim turned from the window to go down the hallway to the bathroom, but just as she opened the door, the victorious houseboy appeared with the passport on a small tray.

"It isn't mine," Kim started to explain, then realized that to an East African she was speaking a foreign language.

"*Asante*," she then said with a smile, using the Swahili word for thank you, which she had learned only yesterday. "*Asante*." She tried to express her gratitude by shaking the boy's hand warmly and repeating the word. He grinned, burst into a flood of Swahili, thrust the passport into her hand, and padded back down the hall.

Kim opened the booklet to check the owner's name.

Vernon W. Bixel, 123 East 91st Street, New York City. Well, she'd return the passport to Mr. Bixel at breakfast. To see what the gentleman looked like, she flipped another page and found, staring up at her, the unmistakable features of Willard, the tourist with the penchant for leopard skins. He was even less attractive in a passport photo than in the flesh, but it was undeniable that he got around. The booklet was filled with visa stamps.

"Kim! Aren't you dressed yet?" Grandy came into the room, looking well-groomed and even quite rested, considering the night's excitement. "Hurry, sweetie! We were due downstairs ten minutes ago."

Willard arrived in the dining room, where coffee was being served, even later than Kim and her grandmother. He had discovered that his passport was missing, and was about to complain to the colonel when Kim approached. "Are you Mr. Vernon Willard Bixel?"

"Yes. Yes, of course."

"I think this is your passport."

Willard looked at Kim suspiciously. "Where did you get it?" he asked, almost snatching it out of her hand.

Kim smiled sweetly. "From a baboon," she replied, and walked away with no further explanation at all.

4

Treetops, for Kim, was a preview of the real drama of a safari. The great herds of buffaloes, streaming through the dusk with the inexorability of a lava flow, whetted her appetite and introduced her to the thrill of seeing animals in the wild.

"It's as though we're in a zoo cage and they're outside," she wrote on a postcard to her parents. "It's all perfectly marvelous but impossible to describe. Nobody can possibly *tell* you what it's like."

Not until the drive across the Athi plains did Kim get into the rhythm that would be repeated, with variations, in the days to come. And even then the strange names on the typed itinerary had no real meaning: Amboseli, Lake Manyara, Ngorongoro, Serengeti, Kilaguni. How could she dream that before she left this vast country these names would beat in her brain like a roll of drums?

52

They would arrive at Amboseli, Peter promised, by midafternoon. To get there they would travel through Masai country. Members of this great tribe still counted their wealth in the number of cattle in their herds, drank cow's blood and milk, and washed in the animals' urine.

Treetops had been in Kikuyu country, where more educable tribesmen tended their little farms, called *shambas*, lived in permanent huts, and sent their children to school. The Masai, in contrast, were nomads, building temporary shelters surrounded by thorn fences, then burning these *manyattas* if the grazing became poor and they wanted to move on.

Kim was anxious to catch a glimpse of such primitive people, but all morning the Land Rover jolted along a rough dirt track across endless plains, and the sun pounded down on scrub growth which could support few animals, let alone people. Such wild things as there were, however, Peter was invariably the first to spot. "There's a secretary bird," he would say, or "Zebras, off in the distance to the right." Kim kept giving false alarms, mistaking a two-eared stump for a warthog and a fallen tree for a rhino. Until her eyes became accustomed to the heaps of red earth, the red termite mounds were especially confusing. Each looked to her like the back of a sleeping gazelle.

Gradually, the landscape changed to a lightly wooded area, the track narrowed, and human footprints appeared in the dust on the borders of the rutted road. A group of women, quite different from any other Africans Kim had seen, were standing, surrounded by children, in the shade of a spreading acacia tree. "Oh, please!" Grandy cried. "I'd love a picture. Do you think they'd let me? Can we stop and ask?"

"Of course." Peter pulled up and everyone slid out of the car, stretching cramped legs and smiling at the group to indicate they wanted to be friendly.

"*Jambo,*" Peter said in greeting.

Kim and her grandmother echoed the Swahili hello, "*Jambo, jambo.*"

Several minutes of conversation followed, accompanied by a great deal of giggling on the part of the women, all of whom had smooth shaven heads and wore heavy bibs of bright-colored beads as well as arm and leg bracelets. One carried a sleeping baby in a sling on her back and had a smooth, moon-shaped face and bright eyes that swept Kim from head to foot.

"She's as interested in you as you are in her," murmured Neil.

"Isn't she handsome!" Kim said. "She can't be more than eighteen, can she?"

"Probably less than that. Masai girls mature early."

All of the women were tall, some standing nearly six feet, and they were uniformly slender. The children, clinging to their mother's long, rust-colored cotton robes, were as shy as gazelles, but the adults seemed unafraid and genuinely amused by the encounter.

Peter completed his bargaining. "They say you may

take their picture, Mrs. Gardiner, if you give them three shillings."

"All right," Grandy agreed. "Kim, find some change, will you?" She began focusing on the little group, in spite of the fact that one toddler, frightened by the unfamiliar camera, had started to cry.

As Kim came forward to hand the coins to Peter, so that he could give them to the woman who seemed to be in command, a small girl reached out and touched her khaki slacks curiously. Like most of the other children, she was quite naked, and her eyes were surrounded by flies, which she completely ignored. Dust powdered her slight body, and bead bracelets clung to her upper arms. The little girl was so appealing that Kim wished she knew some Swahili, but all she could do was repeat *jambo* and smile. Nobody had thought to bring along candy for presents, which was a shame. Perhaps she should buy some sweets if they passed through a market town.

No villages lay along the cross-country route, however, if one discounted the occasional Masai *manyatta* in the distance. Fitting into the landscape like a bird's nest into a tree, each settlement was camouflaged as effectively as a leopard or cheetah sleeping under a bush.

Shortly, the Land Rover's progress was slowed by a herd of cattle, swinging along the road at the urging of a half-grown shepherd. A length of coppery-red cloth caught up and tied on one shoulder was his only garment, and Peter explained that this was in fact the

55

tribal costume, although the lad was still too young to have been initiated, through complicated puberty rites, to the status of a young man.

The road, empty again, stretched straight ahead to the horizon, when two figures carrying lethal-looking spears emerged from the bush far ahead. Peter slowed down. "Masai warriors," he said. "Would you like to stop, Mrs. Gardiner?"

Kim and her grandmother both answered at once, affirmatively, and the Land Rover stopped beside a pair of young men who looked as though they were painted for a fancy-dress ball. One was skinny and quite homely, but the other was strangely handsome. Long-legged, tall, and composed, he stood looking at the party of tourists questioningly. His head, with high cheekbones and an aquiline nose, was as slender as his body, but it was his hair that fascinated Kim. Divided into tufts, each plaited with twine and tied at the ends, it fell in dozens of limp pigtails thickly smeared with a mixture of grease and red ochre. The front plaits dangled over his forehead and the back ones, gathered in a queue, hung down to cover the nape of his neck.

"Our hippies ought to get a glimpse of these characters!" Kim murmured. "Is it safe to get out of the car?"

Both Peter and Neil laughed and nodded. "Quite safe," they replied in unison.

Then Neil added, "Especially if you'd like to buy a spear."

"Oh, I would!" Kim cried at once. "I have a friend in Boston who asked me to try to get one for him." Then she hesitated. "If they're not too expensive."

"What do you call expensive?" Peter asked.

Kim spread her hands. "Five dollars?"

"I think we can do better than that." Peter climbed down from the car, rounded the radiator and leaned against the front fender, getting into conversation in Swahili. The young men answered, first in monosyllables and then with increasing interest, while Mrs. Gardiner reloaded her camera and Kim continued to inspect the warriors covertly. Their arms and bodies were expertly painted with ochre in intricate patterns, and their bare legs were striped in a manner that suggested long socks rising rather absurdly from their bare feet.

Yet there was nothing absurd about the bearing of these Masai warriors. They looked proud and self-contained, as though the status of manhood pleased them, and a sense of humor seemed to enter into their negotiations with Peter, who took each spear into his hands in turn.

The word *simba* kept recurring in the bargaining, which seemed to be starting in earnest. Kim got out of the car, wallet in hand, to inspect her prospective purchase more closely, and her grandmother followed with her camera, which the warriors regarded with a certain reserve.

Peter hefted the second spear and said to Kim, "Four notches is supposed to mean that this has killed four lions. See." He indicated the indentations on the haft.

"How much does he want for it?" Kim inquired with a smile.

"How much, including a picture?" her grandmother asked.

Patiently, Peter returned to the bargaining, and at last appeared to make a deal. "Twenty-five shillings without a picture," he told his clients. "Thirty shillings with."

Kim calculated the cost in American dollars, but her grandmother was faster than she at arithmetic. "That's about three-fifty or four dollars," she murmured. "OK, Kim?"

Kim nodded. "It's a deal."

The money was exchanged, the snapshot taken, and the spear put ceremoniously into Kim's hands. She inspected the carved notches at closer range and asked, jokingly, "Only lions—no leopards?"

Peter translated the question and at once the demeanor of the young warriors changed. Their eyes grew mistrustful, and they shook their heads vehemently. "No leopards!" they insisted in Swahili before turning away.

For lack of a safe and shady picnic spot Mrs. Gardiner's party ate lunch in the car—lukewarm sandwiches, fruit, and soft drinks. The sun, by now, was unmerciful, the dust choking. Kim wiped her perspiring face with a cleansing tissue, which at once became as red as the road.

Imperceptibly, the landscape changed once more, and the Land Rover plunged through a sea of desert vegetation, with leafless trees, rubbed barkless by elephants, making a wasteland of the plain. A few zebras raised a dust cloud in the distance, but straight ahead there was nothing but a dry lake bottom of whitish clay.

"Lake Amboseli—they dig meerschaum here," Peter explained. "In the rainy season we have to go around, but now we can drive straight across."

Off he started over a curious desert where not a blade of grass grew. There was no sign of a road, but the direction was indicated by a maze of tire tracks which snaked across the baked earth.

Far in the distance water shimmered, and Kim cried, "Oh, look!" The prospect of reaching a real lake made her spirits revive.

Peter had to disillusion her. "It's only a mirage, I'm sorry to say."

"A mirage? I've never seen one." Kim remembered all the stories she had read years ago. Men lost in a desert were always crawling toward a water hole that evaporated on their approach. She had half discounted the phenomenon, but the stories must have been true, because the lake ahead disappeared before they quite reached its shores.

A line of trees loomed up, beyond another shining

lake, drawing them on until, almost at the water's edge, the light sucked the mirage up into the shimmering air. Dust poured over the Land Rover in thick clouds, and even with the windows rolled up it got into Kim's eyes, ears, and nose. Grandy began to cough, and Peter turned sympathetically. "Hang on another half hour and we'll be there."

"Don't worry about me," Kim's grandmother said gamely. "I'm just fine!"

Late that afternoon Kim came into the lounge of the safari lodge to buy some postage stamps. So far as she was concerned, the discomforts of the long drive were forgotten, but her grandmother was still coughing, her chest heavy as if with bronchitis. Although she had been a very good sport all through the day, she had finally succumbed to the need to take a really long nap.

After leaving her postcards at the desk for mailing, Kim felt rather at loose ends. She wandered across the lobby and picked up an abandoned Nairobi newspaper, in which a first-page story, bearing a Treetops dateline, was concerned with the remarkable bongo fight.

Another news item rated a good deal more space, however. *Leopard Skins Are Target of Powerful Poaching Ring,* announced the headline. Kim sank down on a low chair and read on.

"A powerful criminal organization," stated the lead sentence, "is supplying the leopard skin market in

Kenya and Tanzania, according to influential wildlife investigators here." An official of the East African Wildlife Society was quoted as saying, "It's the middleman I'd really like to nab. Leopard is now the most valuable pelt in the world, and there is definitely a wide organization at work in the illegal skin trade."

"What's so fascinating?" asked Neil Abercrombie, jackknifing his thin body into a chair opposite. "You look completely absorbed."

"I'm interested in this poaching business," Kim replied. Folding the newspaper to pinpoint the story, she handed it to him. "Read this."

Neil took the paper and glanced down the columns of type politely, as though he had read it all before. "It's a big problem."

"It ought to be stopped!"

"My father would certainly agree with you. Got any ideas?"

"Certainly. Catch the poachers and put them in jail."

Neil grinned. "Poachers are hard to catch, partly because most of the native Africans don't consider it wrong to kill wild animals."

"But leopards are getting so scarce," Kim complained.

Neil agreed. "Dad says if something isn't done soon, we'll be in the same shape as Somalia. It says here that eighty percent of the Somali leopards have been killed since 1960. Pretty shocking, isn't it?"

"Terrible!" Kim said. "You know, I'm beginning to

understand why Grandy's so hipped on conservation. But I wish these wildlife people could dream up a more exciting word. Conservation just doesn't send me, somehow. There should be a really dramatic way of saying the same thing."

Neil chuckled appreciatively and reached up to scratch the tip of his sunburned nose. "Leave it alone," Kim advised. "You'll look like a peeled tomato if you aren't careful."

Instead of offending him, the comment seemed to tickle Neil's sense of humor. He had relaxed appreciably during this hard day's drive, probably because Kim's graphic report of the excitement at Treetops had provided enough leverage to break the conversational ice. As he became less abrupt and didactic, Kim unbent too. The wild grandeur of this country and its animals made it seem silly to harbor a grudge against a fellow human being. Besides, on a journey crammed with unknowns, four people sharing a small car were in a vulnerable position. Either they had to learn to get along amicably with one another or settle for being thoroughly miserable.

Fortunately Peter Kent was a catalyst. He acted as teacher and protector, as well as guide. And the sheer wonder of East Africa, with its extremes and contrasts, carried everyone far back in time and created a changed awareness in which personality conflicts were simply too unimportant to be borne.

"Grandy's going to skip a game run this afternoon,"

Kim said to Neil after a while. "She's still coughing a lot and I think she's tired."

"I'll tell Peter," Neil said. "He's trying to put through a couple of phone calls to Nairobi, and maybe he'd prefer it if you and I went off alone."

"Alone? Are you allowed?"

"Certainly," Neil told her, sounding surprised by the question. "I often drive for Dad, and I know Amboseli like the back of my hand."

Riding up front in the Land Rover proved to be rather fun. Neil was a good driver, and the slow, steady cruising along dirt tracks and across grassland was pleasant. Looking for game, Kim kept alert. She felt very proud of herself when she was the first to spot two lions and a lioness sleeping in the tall grass. They raised their heads at the car's approach, yawned lazily, and went back to sleep. Neil cut the motor and waited for five minutes or so, but then decided to move on. "They're obviously not hungry," he told Kim, "so they're apt to lie there for hours."

The late afternoon light was soft and hazy, so hazy that not a glimpse of Mt. Kilimanjaro, with the snow-crowned cone Peter had promised as an Amboseli bonus, could be seen. Occasionally, in the distance, a plume of dust indicated the presence of another car, but for the most part the countryside was occupied only by the animals whose forebears had lived there for centuries.

Kim started to make a count. Headed by the three lions, her list grew to include two rhinos, a solitary elephant, and a group of five buffaloes. "I'd love to see a leopard or a cheetah," she said.

"So would I," Neil replied, then repeated a phrase which was becoming familiar to Kim. "They're very hard to see."

Among umbrella acacias the car rocked down a rutted track to a small, thorn-margined river, easy to ford. Behind the haze the sun was dropping, igniting clouds and turning them fiery. Overhead, however, Kim noticed that the sky was black.

"We'll turn back soon," Neil said. "We may have a thunderstorm."

Because it wasn't the rainy season, Kim had anticipated a succession of dry, warm days, but she was learning that mornings were apt to be gray and cool, noontimes hot, and a sudden shower could be expected at any time. As Neil inched the car across the rocky riverbed, she glanced up unconcernedly, and a few minutes later all thought of the coming storm was erased from her mind. Simultaneously, she and Neil spotted a leopard in a tree.

He was lying on a long branch with his kill, the remnants of a gazelle referred to generally as a "Tommy." The leopard was smaller than Kim had envisioned but even more beautiful, sleek and silky, with an aristocratic small head and a spotted pelt that on a clear day would have blended perfectly with sunlight dancing on the leaves.

Neil drove a little closer, then switched off the ignition and whispered to Kim, "We're in luck!"

Quietly the pair climbed onto the seat and raised themselves to the open hatch, from which they could get a better view. The leopard saw them, because he stopped eating for a moment and turned his head, but Kim and Neil might as well have been a pair of nearby saplings for all he cared. Crouched securely on his limb, he continued his meal undisturbed.

"That kill can't be more than a day old," Neil whispered knowledgeably. "He may still be there in the morning. We'll have to come back."

"Oh yes! Grandy should see him," Kim murmured. It seemed a pity that, on this very special occasion of finding their first leopard, her grandmother wasn't along. Raising her binoculars, she inspected the leopard more closely—a mere hundred pounds of gorgeous cat, but with steel muscles and the intelligent, calculating look of a conqueror.

"His Swahili name is *chui*," Neil said softly. "For my money he's the real king of beasts. He never travels with a crowd. He lives and dies alone, as a king must. And, pound for pound, he's the strongest animal on earth."

"Stronger than a lion?" Kim asked.

"And braver," said Neil, nodding. "Compared to a leopard, a lion is a good-natured, indolent family man who lets his women do the killing and sleeps twenty hours out of every twenty-four. May I borrow your glasses?" Neil carefully refocused. "Good grief, isn't he beautiful! Even though I live in this country, I've seen only half a dozen leopards in my whole life!"

This boyish admission both surprised Kim and made her feel very fortunate. Then a bright flash of lightning, coming from directly overhead, distracted her attention from the great cat.

A thunderclap followed, and suddenly it began to rain. No big drops plopped down in warning, as at home. The clouds simply ripped apart, dumping their contents on the earth, and Neil slammed the hatch shut several seconds too late.

"We'd better get back across that river," he said, quickly starting the motor and swinging the car around.

The stream was no more than half a mile away, and the rocky riverbed had been almost dry, so Kim wasn't unduly concerned. She got out a handkerchief and began swabbing the steamy windshield, first on Neil's side, then on her own. Outside, the water poured and pounded on the track, turning dust to mud in a matter of seconds. Neil handled the four-wheel drive expertly, but it was impossible to avoid slipping and sloshing through the quagmire. "Hold on tight," he advised.

Kim turned sideways and clung to the back of the seat. The car lurched along from one side of the track to the other, as the mud seemed to be turning to heavy grease. Spinning the steering wheel, Neil somehow managed to keep moving, and soon the river could be heard rushing past. From a gentle stream it had turned into a torrent.

"A flash flood," Neil muttered, "coming down from the mountain. It could get worse before it eases off. I'll have to try to get through."

Kim hung on, more excited than frightened, as the Land Rover skidded down an all but invisible bank. Water swirled up over the wheels and through the floor, but the engine kept running, while stones gripped the tires and gave Neil traction. "With luck, we're going to make it," he said.

"I'll cross my fingers," Kim suggested, although she wasn't in the least superstitious.

Thirty seconds later both luck and magic abruptly failed. Knowing that only a spurt of speed could pull the car up the far bank, Neil accelerated. The engine roared and the Land Rover leaped forward, but for a moment only. The front wheels kept spinning and the rear ones settled inexorably into the mire.

5

The squared-off hood of the car was pointing upward toward a rift in the clouds, and Kim was lying back against the tilted seat with her knees almost in front of her nose.

"Well, that ties it," Neil said in disgust. "I'll never get her loose from this muck."

He switched off the engine and pocketed the keys. Then, ignoring the fact that the rain was slackening but had not stopped, he managed to get the door open and ease his way out.

At once he was up to his ankles in glue. Kim slid across the seat and, with one hand clinging to the wheel, leaned out to watch him explore the full extent of the catastrophe.

"Not a chance. She's in over the hubcaps."

"What are we going to do?"

"Walk," Neil said. "We're no more than two miles from the lodge."

"Walk?" Kim's voice rose in alarm. A large, hand-lettered sign at the gate had warned: *Any person found on foot outside the compound fence will be subject to 1,000 shillings fine.* She remembered other signs, too. *Elephants have right of way,* for one. Posted at the entrance to the game reserve, it had seemed amusing rather than serious. "What about all this business of staying in your car?" she asked Neil. "Isn't walking dangerous?"

"We have a gun," he reminded her, slogging through the mud as though each foot weighed a ton. "It's in that case stowed in the back. Do you think you can reach it?"

Kim squirmed around and clambered into the back seat, leaned over and managed to unstrap the gun case, providentially fastened well above the waterline. Overhead the fragment of blue sky was touched with color, and the clouds were blowing rapidly to the east. The rain had almost stopped, although the swirling red water was still rising. It was obvious that staying in the car could be even more risky than taking their chances on foot, and that walking might be the alternative to drowning.

Gingerly, Kim handed the gun case to Neil. Is that thing loaded? she wanted to ask. And do you know how to use it? She watched him strip off the canvas covering with both questions on the tip of her tongue, but Neil, acting with unexpected authority, said, "Come on. Let's get out of here."

Kim glanced ruefully at her new safari boots before she slid down from the tilted seat. Never again would she see the soft leather in its pristine state. In fact, as she plowed through the red mud in Neil's wake, she wondered if ever again she would see the boots at all. Each felt like a leaden weight, and she had to lift her knees high in order to take every forward step. Neil reached back and offered a hand, and together they slipped and slid up the greasy red bank, pulling themselves to the top by grabbing at firmly rooted tufts of coarse grass.

"Do you know the way, Neil?"

"Of course. That part's easy." He was checking the gun as he spoke, clicking the safety and sighting along the barrel.

Kim glanced back at the roaring river, fringed with glistening reeds and trees heavy with wet leaves. The mist was drifting eastward after the clouds, and slowly, in the far distance, the mountain was emerging. "Oh, look!" she cried in spontaneous delight.

The white snow cliffs at the summit appeared first, hanging on a cloud platform sixteen thousand feet high. As unreal as a mirage, the scene was lit for one unearthly minute by the setting sun. "Is there skiing up there?" Kim asked.

Neil groaned. "Can't you think of anything but skiing? You're in Africa!"

Since Kim could not remember having mentioned

skiing since the evening on which she and Neil first had met, she felt insulted. "It would make a wonderful advertisement," she insisted. "Skiing on the equator. Why not?"

"I'll tell you some other time." Neil kept on walking, although Kim could scarcely tear herself away. Starting to plod along, she looked over her shoulder to watch the upper slopes of the mountain until their outlines became clear. For a few minutes Kilimanjaro hovered like a conical crown in the sky, ablaze with color. Then the light died, and the rock cliffs turned to a dull gray.

"Step out, Kim, unless you want to get caught here in the dark."

With a shiver of foreboding, Kim began to slog along as fast as her mud-clogged boots would carry her. Walking was easier in the grass that bordered the track than on the track itself, and she followed Neil dutifully along whatever path he chose.

The clearing skies and the approach of night had flushed birds and animals into activity. Wood pigeons called to one another in a melancholy cadence: *kikuyu, kikuyu.* A dik-dik, the smallest and most fragile of all gazelles, leaped across the track after a single startled glance at the strangers who had invaded his territory. In a small grove of trees long-tailed Colobus monkeys swung in flashes of black and white, bending the creaking branches to peer down curiously and chatter among themselves. Kim could spare them only a passing glance. Keeping up with Neil was not easy.

71

The track branched at a triangle of woodland and Neil took the left-hand path without hesitation. From behind a thick-trunked baobab tree, reddened by the rubbing of elephants, stepped a lone Masai carrying a six-foot spear. As surprised to see Neil and Kim as they were to see him, he halted abruptly and stood quite still, one foot tucked up against the opposite thigh in a cranelike posture, waiting for them to approach.

"*Jambo*," Neil said.

"*Jambo*," came the usual reply.

In a mixture of Swahili and Masai, Neil explained their predicament. Kim caught only a couple of words, evidently untranslatable—Land Rover and lodge.

The Masai was a taciturn fellow. He looked Neil right in the eye but seemed uninterested. Kim, standing by, had time to appraise him. Apparently he was a warrior, although his red ochre paint had been drenched by the shower and was running down his legs and arms in small rivulets. The length of cloth twisted around his body was wet and clinging, but the soaking apparently had left him undismayed. When Neil said good-bye and Kim parroted, *kwaheri*, he started off toward the river they had just left.

"Will he steal anything from the Land Rover?" Kim asked.

"Let him. There's nothing there he could possibly want except an empty picnic basket."

"What about the spare tire?"

Neil shook his head. "The Masai have no interest in the white man's world."

"Humph," Kim grunted. "The white man's world is going to look pretty good to me, if we ever get back to it. Will that rifle you're carrying kill an elephant?"

Neil cast a disdainful glance over his shoulder. "Hardly."

"What do we do if we meet one?"

"Stand still. That goes for any wild animal. For Pete's sake, stand still."

Hoping she wouldn't have to put this advice to the test, Kim tried to walk a little faster. "I'd do better without these boots," she suggested.

But Neil simply muttered, "Snakes."

Not a streamer of color remained in the sky. The tropical night, equally as long as the day, always came quickly. The birds had quieted down, but new sounds assaulted Kim's ears. Baboons screamed and barked in the distance, hyenas wailed like sirens, and from the direction of the river a lion roared.

Kim's heart began to pound. "How much farther?"

"Less than a mile now."

Neil's pace increased. "Keep talking," he advised in a loud voice. "It's just as well to let the animals know we're here."

"What shall I talk about?" Naturally, Kim felt tongue-tied.

"Anything. What's the skiing like in New England?"

"Good."

"I've always thought it would be fun to learn to ski, but of course I've never had the opportunity."

"That's too bad," Kim said.

"For a girl who can talk about nothing *but* skiing for twenty minutes at a time, you're a dud at this sort of game," Neil complained.

"Don't be so critical. And besides, it isn't a game. That's the trouble." Kim glanced up at the thin crescent moon in the slate-colored sky and asked, "How soon will it be really dark?"

"Not for ten or fifteen minutes. We should make it back by then."

"That's ducky."

"What did you say?"

"Nothing. It's American slang."

The lion roared again, and Kim shivered. If it had been possible, she would have started to run. "Take it easy," Neil advised, "and remember that wild animals usually won't attack humans, unless they're provoked."

"How do I know they won't find me provoking?"

The attempt at a joke fell flat, but it didn't matter. At that moment, across a stretch of open plain, the lights of the safari lodge winked and flickered. Then the headlights of a Land Cruiser cut into the path along which the pair were hurrying. Neil permitted himself a long, heartfelt sigh of relief. "I expected Peter to start looking for us long before this," he said.

The next morning, by the time Kim and her grandmother had dressed and swallowed hot cups of sugary tea, a truck from the lodge had rescued the Land Rover, which was found, as Neil had predicted, quite intact.

He had taken a dressing down from Peter with surprising decency, Kim felt, considering the fact that he had behaved with a good deal of common sense and courage. "Honestly, Peter, it wasn't Neil's fault," she had said, seeking to defend him. "How could he know there'd be a real flash flood?"

"If he'd been looking at the sky instead of at the leopard, he could have told a storm was coming. You had just crossed a river. Two and two make four, or they'd better, if you're out with a client at sundown in the highlands."

This morning, however, the incident was closed. They were off to see if the leopard was still crouched in the same tree, guarding his kill, and the earlier they could reach the spot the more chance they had of finding him.

Grandy, rested and enthusiastic once more, was in top form. She sniffed happily at the freshly washed air and ohed and ahed at the spectacular sight of snow-capped, cone-shaped Kilimanjaro, standing forty miles away in naked grandeur against a clear blue sky. "Hemingway's mountain," she breathed. "I was afraid I'd never see it!"

Once more the safari leader drove. Because it promised to be rough crossing the river, Peter suggested that Mrs. Gardiner sit up front. Kim and Neil, riding in the back seat, had an opportunity to exchange glances and an occasional whispered comment as they retraced the route they had traveled so riskily on foot.

"Here's where we met the Masai, remember?"

Neil nodded. "He certainly wasn't very helpful. I wanted him to stick with us until we got to the lodge."

"And he refused?" Kim had not been aware of this. "I wonder why?"

Shrugging, Neil said, "We'll never know." Then he stared out of the window thoughtfully and added, after an interval, "I hope."

Although it was an ambiguous remark, Kim didn't challenge it. The river was straight ahead, and she was eager to see if it had gone down enough to permit them to cross, because she did want her grandmother to get a picture of the one leopard they might have the opportunity of photographing. Fortunately the flow of water was reduced, once more, to a trickle. The roaring red flood following the thunderstorm seemed like a figment of the imagination. Peter rocked the car across the stony bed as gently as Neil had done on the previous afternoon, then skidded up the bank on the other side.

The road there was still too muddy to be passable, but the Land Rover, which sometimes seemed to have a life of its own, ran cleverly through the scrub growth on the edge of the track, slapping at the low-growing bushes and maintaining traction without difficulty.

Neil ran the window down on his side of the car

and leaned out, looking up at the sky. Kim giggled. "Not a cloud!" she teased in an undertone. Then she saw the vultures soaring above the trees to plummet down in a thicket less than half a mile away.

Peter saw them a second later, and his mouth became grim. "Looks like a fresh kill. I hope it isn't your leopard, Neil."

"He may have abandoned the antelope he was eating," Kim suggested hopefully. "They may be working on that."

"I doubt it," Peter said. "Mysteriously enough, vultures seldom touch a leopard's kill, even though *chui* himself may be sound asleep in a cave half a mile away."

In a few minutes the repulsive, carrion-eating birds became visible in even greater numbers, stationed on treetops or descending into the briars. "Got the right tree spotted, Neil?" Peter asked.

"It's up ahead on the left," muttered Neil unhappily. "Doggone!"

Kim's stomach suddenly felt squeamish as the car heaved across the track. A flock of a dozen or more of the scavengers were tearing at a stripped pillow of red meat, while above, in the crotch of the tree she remembered so vividly, hung the remains of the leopard's putrefying meal.

Peter braked to a stop but didn't cut the engine. He simply sat and stared in silence at the unappetizing sight.

"Skinned," Neil finally said.

"Poachers?" Grandy questioned. "Is this what poachers do?" She sounded horrified.

"It is most certainly what poachers do," Peter aroused himself to answer soberly. "If ever there was an object lesson, this is it."

In the back seat Kim was silent, twisting the strap on her binoculars. She was seeing not the mangled corpse covered by birds of prey, but a vision of dappled sunlight on the sleek, silken coat of the real king of beasts who, in all his majestic strength, still was unable to conquer the beast in man.

Tears, which she was unable to control, slipped down her smooth young cheeks. Peter turned back toward the lodge. Grandy huddled in a corner, looking diminished. Awkwardly, after a little while, Neil reached out and started to stroke Kim's hand.

6

Breakfast at the lodge was followed by a long, dusty drive, capped by an interminable wait at the border between Kenya and Tanzania, where three zebra-striped Volkswagen buses had beaten Peter to the entrance gate.

Kim, by now accepting the fact that her grandmother had permanently usurped Neil's position on the front seat of the Land Rover, jounced along in the rear, making little conversation as she tried to keep her knees from bumping against Neil's. At Lake Manyara she dutifully admired thousands of pink flamingos riding on the smooth surface of the water, watched a flight of comical pelicans, and raised sufficient enthusiasm to satisfy her grandmother when Peter, driving through a wooded section, discovered two lions asleep in the branches of a tree. Her mind was still on the murdered leopard. Such things shouldn't be allowed to happen, she fumed inwardly. Somebody ought to *do* something!

Because she suspected the spear-carrying Masai of killing the leopard, Kim began to find the red-ochred tribesmen distasteful. Even a teen-aged shepherd driving his skinny cattle along the trace seemed far from innocent. Who knew how soon he would exchange his staff for a poison-tipped spear?

"Don't be silly, darling. Most of these people are completely harmless," Grandy argued persuasively, but Kim continued to shake her head.

"I'm going to write a term paper for social studies on leopard poaching," she decided. "I'll get Neil to help me collect all the facts."

Mrs. Gardiner heartily approved of the project. "Very good!" she cried enthusiastically. "I'll help too." When they arrived at the Lake Manyara Hotel, she unearthed from her suitcase half a dozen issues of a journal on conservation. "As a start, you might read these."

Kim leafed through the top magazine, but the printed word seemed far less enthralling than real life, and she wasn't sorry when it was time to go to dinner. The dining room was unusually crowded, however, and the food was mediocre. Peter and Neil were not with them, since they had eaten earlier, so Kim and her grandmother waited for the various courses to appear and looked around.

80

Long tables had been set for the members of Zebra Tours, and at one of these Mrs. Gardiner discovered a familiar face. "Why, there's Mopsy!" she said with a chuckle. "And she still looks as though she were dressed for lunch at a country club."

Also, as Kim could see when the group started to leave the room, Mopsy was still clutching her big straw bag. Spying Mrs. Gardiner from the corner of her eye, she tacked over to her table and cried, "I knew we'd run into you sooner or later! Are you enjoying yourselves?"

"Enormously," said Mrs. Gardiner. "And you?"

"Well, it's pretty hectic. All these one-night stands."

"Where have you been, so far?"

"Oh, dear me, the names are so strange it's hard to remember. Except for the Mt. Kenya Safari Club. That's perfectly beautiful. You'd just love the birds, Ellen, you really would." She started to enumerate. "Crested cranes, black swans, peacocks, secretary birds. You can walk right up close to them."

"Naturally." Mrs. Gardiner's tone expressed a certain coolness. "I understand they've all had their wings clipped."

"Have they really?" Mopsy's eyes opened wider. "I didn't notice." As she spoke, Kim stifled a smile. She strongly doubted that Mrs. Collins was the noticing type.

The two women chatted a few minutes longer, during which time Mrs. Gardiner was persuaded to join

Mopsy and her traveling companions for coffee on the verandah. Kim excused herself and wandered through the lounge toward the entrance, edging past the luggage of some late arrivals who were still checking in. Outside, in the soft African night, floodlights were trained on the driveway, where buses and safari cars were ranged in a long, ragged row. Several drivers were standing around chatting, a professional hunter among them, and in the sky above danced thousands of diamond-bright stars.

Kim leaned against the cool stone wall of the lodge and tried to identify some of the star patterns that twinkled so strongly. She spotted a few familiar constellations, but they were displaced a quarter across the bowl of the sky from where she had been accustomed to seeing them at home. The handle of the Big Dipper was pointing downward at a steep angle, but the polestar was too near the horizon to be seen. New England was certainly a long distance away!

When she glanced back at the driveway again, the pattern had changed, like a set replacing another in a country dance. One of the drivers had walked down past the lamppost, where he was soon joined by a burly man who emerged from one of the guest cottages near the lodge. A conference ensued. From the shadows Kim watched idly, then with increasing interest, because something about the man's thick neck and close-cropped hair seemed familiar. Although she couldn't get a glimpse of his face, she was sure she had seen that heavy body before. When he stepped momentarily into the light, his back was toward her, but she watched curiously as he extracted a wallet from his trousers pocket and took out what appeared to be a number of bills.

These he counted into the driver's hand, then turned along a path near the fence and walked off in the direction from which he had come. Kim still couldn't get a glimpse of his face, but the feeling that she had seen him before was strengthened by something about his gait. He seemed, almost, to be stealing away.

The driver, meanwhile, was sauntering forward, whistling softly between his teeth. He approached one of the Zebra buses and leaned in to open the glove compartment, stuffed something inside, then locked it carefully before closing the Volkswagen's windows against the night's dew. Although, in the darkness, black features melted into the background, for several moments the lamp highlighted a sharp chin, a rather flat nose, and a long welt that ran down the man's right cheek. Kim would be certain to recognize him if she ever saw him again, but why she cared she could not explain, even to herself.

Kim and her grandmother were awakened at five o'clock the next morning, so that they could get an early start and reach the Ngorongoro Crater before the day was so far advanced that interesting animals would be scarce. Yawning, Kim gulped a cup of tea, pulled on slacks and shirt, and crammed her night things into a flight bag too full to zip shut.

Peter greeted them quietly and they drove off through the dawn, frightening a dik-dik who stood staring for a split second out of white-ringed purple eyes, bright with vigilance. Then it bounded into the undergrowth and was gone.

"I like the dik-diks best. They look like toy antelopes," Kim said.

"You said the same thing yesterday, and the day before that," Neil reminded her.

"And she'll say it again tomorrow." Mrs. Gardiner laughed. She turned to pat her granddaughter's khaki-clad knee. "Never mind, dear. We all love you in spite of the fact that you tend to repeat yourself."

Kim didn't mind being teased. Their small party had settled into a casual camaraderie which permitted such amusements. Peter was still the father figure, Neil the luggage toter and general handyman, Mrs. Gardiner the diminutive autocrat, but Kim's role was changing. From being the grandchild along for the ride, she was becoming a passionate champion of any and all of the wild animals.

Especially of the leopard. "What should we call her, a leopardophile?" asked Peter as he drove up a pass to the rim of the crater. The sun was climbing and the heat was rising, so he was anxious to reach the top before the landscape, marvelously etched in blacks and greens by the early morning light, dissolved into a hazy panorama blurred by the midday glare.

Kim felt as though she were driving up a road to the sky. Each curve led to another stretch of bone-rattling washboard, and she clung to one of the car's overhead struts with one hand while she crooked an elbow over the back of the seat. Then suddenly the four of them were piling out of the car to stand on the ridge, which offered the first sweeping view of the crater. Two thousand feet below lay a circular floor of celadon green dotted with animals no bigger than ants. Near the center of this great bowl was a broad, delphinium blue lake, and twelve miles away, on the opposite wall, forests climbed to the rim, furry and sleek as an animal's pelt.

"Ngorongoro," Mrs. Gardiner breathed. "Until now it has been just a word."

Kim stood silent. All proportion was lost. The air quivered with light, the wind was cold, and the sun was very close. Iridescent birds flashed overhead, and on the crater floor herds of indistinguishable animals seemed to be standing quite still.

"Let's go," Peter said. "It's even better below."

The road down the rim looked impassable, steep as a flight of stairs but far more hazardous. Rocking and groaning, the Land Rover edged down in low gear. Guard rails were unheard of in this country, and the drop to the crater floor was sheer. Nobody tried to talk, least of all Peter. Maneuvering skillfully, he somehow kept the car on the one-way track down the side of the cliff.

Half an hour later Kim breathed a sigh of relief. They were down! Down to a plain dancing beneath a haze of heat. The animals sorted themselves out; here a herd of wildebeests, there a solitary rhinoceros seeking the shade of a clump of trees with tops like feather dusters, in the distance a group of Thompson's gazelles, an alert buck guarding his does and their young.

"This can't have changed in a hundred thousand years." Mrs. Gardiner spoke softly and with awe.

"Does anybody live down here?" Kim asked. "I mean anybody except animals?"

"Only a couple of Masai families," Peter replied. "Later on we'll visit a *manyatta,* if you like. They'll even invite you inside the village if you give them a few shillings."

He drove, seemingly at random, across short-cropped green grass dotted with starlike white wild-flowers. The lake glistened over to the right, and straight ahead the volcano's ancient floor terminated abruptly in an escarpment rising as sheerly as the wall of a room. Kim turned slowly around toward the rear of the car to follow with her eyes the perimeter of the crater and there, almost hidden in clouds on the rim above, lay the tourist lodge. It seemed anachronistic, even from this distance. Only down here were the surroundings properly placed in time.

Bearded wildebeests, which Kim had learned to call

gnus when she saw them as a child in American zoos, were grazing near the flat white shores of the soda lake. Groups of zebras, less panicky than others Peter had approached, wandered near the car and seemed almost friendly. "If I were an animal, I'd want to be a zebra," Mrs. Gardiner said. "They're so decorative."

"Sh!" Peter cautioned. "Look ahead, over to the left."

There, half hidden by waving grass, was a black-maned lion, head held high, contemplating the car from wide-open amber eyes.

"Bert Lahr!" Kim gasped, lowering her voice to a whisper. "It's got to be Bert Lahr. Remember the Cowardly Lion in the Wizard of Oz?"

Peter cut the motor. "He's guarding a kill. See." Pointing, the hunter guided the eyes of his companions to a half-devoured carcass of a wildebeest, then to the top branches of a nearby baobab tree. "The vultures are waiting for the leftovers."

Kim shuddered. She hated the fierce-looking, lappet-faced birds, hungrily anticipating the feast to come. Folded into their wings as though they were clutching black capes around their bodies, they looked menacing and gluttonous.

"The lion won't let them near until he's finished," Peter explained. "Then, like as not, his wives and children will take a turn. Finally the hyenas and vultures feed. The marabou storks can't tear the meat, so they eat last of all."

Aware of Kim's revulsion, her grandmother turned

and said, "In a way it's not really horrible. It's perfectly natural, using dead animals as food and leaving the earth clean and fresh."

Peter smiled and nodded. "The hyenas eat even the bones. You can tell by the coating of lime on their white moustaches. Nothing is wasted here."

Kim got out her pocket notebook and scribbled something in it. "Peebee will be pleased with me," she said with a grin.

"Who's Peebee?" Neil asked.

"Miss Peabody, our headmistress at school."

School! The word sounded so strange on her tongue that Kim was startled. Civilization was like an impossible dream down here. The knowledge that she might well—right now!—be skiing in New England seemed ridiculous.

Peter moved the car on, to skirt the wall of the crater, where thin streams of clear water poured down to form pools or marshland and finally to flow into the lake. He drove for an hour or more, never out of sight of animals, past blowing wild flowers, groves of trees and miniature waterfalls, then climbed a low hill and parked in the shade of a spreading fig tree. "It's safe to get out here," he said. "This is a good place to have lunch."

Everyone sat on the grass and looked over the dancing heat haze while they ate sandwiches and tilted bottles of lukewarm soft drinks to their lips. Then they piled into the Land Rover again and drove across country, past a herd of grazing Masai cattle, to a thorn-hedged enclosure that was invisible from a few hundred yards away.

"When the herd is out grazing, the Masai leave a space in the hedge open," Neil explained. "But at night they shut themselves in with another bunch of thorn."

Kim could see two figures, tall and motionless, watching the approach of the Land Rover. One man was past middle age and tall, even for a Masai. He held a long spear, and his earth-brown cape flapped around muscular legs. He had an air of command about him, and didn't walk forward as Peter braked to a stop but waited for the hunter to get out and approach with the usual greeting of *jambo.*

"*Jambo,*" he then said, and to Kim's surprise, shook hands. His smile, white-toothed except for a couple of missing incisors, was friendly, and he seemed to know Peter by sight if not by name.

The exchange of greetings apparently indicated to the hidden occupants of the *manyatta* that it was safe to appear. Women and children, accompanied by a couple of young men, drifted across the red earth to the car. They stood staring, while Kim and her grandmother stared back, nodding and smiling in an attempt to reassure and to camouflage their curiosity.

Neil got out, leaving the car door open, and approached one of the young men, while Kim tried to memorize the marvelous adornments. The girls' necks were encircled with concentric rings of bright blue and red beads, their arms were heavily braceleted, and their ears were pierced, the big holes temporarily plugged with corks.

Everyone had great hanging earlobes, Kim noticed. Most of the men and women wore earrings, which brushed their shoulders; the apertures from which they were hung were as large as eggs and obviously the fashion, like leis in Hawaii or Afro hairdos in the United States. She was so fascinated she could almost ignore the flies and the heat.

Peter finished his conversation with the man, who was evidently the chief, and strolled back to the car. "You can get out and take pictures," he said to Mrs. Gardiner, "and you can even go inside and take a look at the huts, but the cost has gone up to twenty shillings." With a wry grin he added, "Ngorongoro isn't quite as out of this world as it looks."

Mrs. Gardiner replied with a smile and a nod. "Interested, Kim?"

"Of course!"

Following her grandmother, Kim crossed the open space to meet the headman, who shook her hand courteously and repeated *jambo* several times. Neil was talking with the young Masai he had approached earlier, who seemed to understand English and could even communicate in a sort of repetitious dialect. She glanced at the fellow curiously, wondering what the pair were discussing, and decided that the Masai looked a little flashy, compared with the rest of the villagers. He was wearing a pair of soiled khaki pants instead of a robe, and his grin, which had something sly about it, displayed a large city-made gold tooth.

Mrs. Gardiner was busy with her camera, focusing on the children and their mothers, while Peter indicated to Kim that she could come through the opening in the six-foot-thick *boma*, made of two fences of saplings driven into the ground, with the space between filled with cut thorn.

"Hapana simba," said the chief proudly, and Kim nodded, understanding. No lion could get in here!

The ground in the center of the compound was trampled and churned by the hooves of cattle, whose dung had been used to plaster and roof four huts built close to the walls. The chief, who had grunted a happy *asante* over Mrs. Gardiner's paper money, now appeared positively cordial. He led Kim over to the door of a hut and indicated that she might go inside.

Curiosity and a sense of courtesy made her want to accept, but the smell was dreadful. She hesitated a moment, then ducked her head and walked bravely through the low doorway into a sort of vestibule where spears were stacked against the wall, then on into an inside room so dark that for a time she could only stand and blink. Then her eyes picked out a young woman sitting on a pallet nursing a sleepy baby, while an ancient, wrinkled crone stood in the background leaning on a stick.

The baby was beautiful and quite naked, except for bead rings on his middle fingers with bridles that secured the rings to bead bracelets on his wrists. Kim smiled and walked over to admire the child more closely, but the young woman, apparently misunderstanding her intention, drew back in fright. Quick as a snake, she slithered over the pallet, disturbing a coverlet of the same red-brown cloth in which she was dressed. The old woman spoke suddenly and sharply, and at the same moment Kim realized that the binoculars hanging around her neck had alarmed the girl. Fright, however, had now given way to a new concern. Holding the baby in one arm, the mother was desperately trying to restore the cotton covering to a pile of folded leopard skins.

Kim caught only a glimpse of the spotted hides, but the evidence was unmistakable. So, also, was the fact that the old woman wanted to be rid of the visitor. She came hobbling toward Kim, shooing her out as she would a stray chicken or an overly curious dog.

Peter was waiting on the threshold, Mrs. Gardiner was involved in picture taking, and Neil was still talking to the youth in Western pants. Not three minutes had passed, yet Kim felt that an hour could have gone by. She was upset, and her face showed her distress. She wanted to tell Peter, or Neil, or at least her grandmother about her discovery, but at that moment her attention was caught by a car approaching in a plume of dust. It was a green Toyota safari wagon, which pulled up within a few yards of where Peter had parked.

Two men emerged, a black driver and a white man with a bull neck, wearing an expensive, sweat-stained shirt. The chief seemed to recognize the pair and walked over to greet them.

"We'd better be getting along," Peter said to Kim, and started toward the car.

Kim followed reluctantly. She didn't recognize the driver, but the white man had a familiar face, thoroughly unpleasant. He reached into the Toyota, took out a hat, and placed it well back on his perspiring forehead. Suddenly Kim remembered where she had seen him before—in the shop in Nairobi where she had gone with her grandmother to buy safari clothes.

The scene flooded her mind as though she had witnessed it yesterday—the Indian and the foreigner trying on hats, the entrance of the curly-haired, leathery man who had identified himself as John Sanderson, and the silent stealing away. . . .

Stealing away! She looked more closely. The thick neck, the close-cropped hair. The silhouette was surely the one she had seen last night under the arc lamp!

"Peter!" Kim grabbed the hunter's arm. "Look at that man. Do you recognize him?"

"Never saw him before in my life."

"I did. In Nairobi."

Peter shrugged. "Everybody hits the big city sooner or later. Why are you interested?"

7

Kim couldn't think of a reply that would sound valid. "I think he looks suspicious," she blurted. "And, Peter, there are leopard skins inside the hut."

Peter glanced at her sharply. "How do you know?"

"I saw them. Honestly."

"There aren't many leopards left, down in this crater. Maybe they were zebra hides."

Kim shook her head stubbornly. "I'm sure."

Peter opened the car door and helped her inside rather brusquely. "Better forget you saw them," he advised. "The Masai are a very primitive tribe, who live by their own rules. There's no use trying to tangle with them. Even the authorities are wary these days." He beckoned rather impatiently to Mrs. Gardiner and Neil, who were lagging behind.

"But, Peter, you said killing leopards was against the law."

"Sure it is, but you're not a police officer." He got into the driver's seat and slammed the door, locking it. "Incidentally, neither am I."

Kim was shocked. She had assumed that Peter's code of ethics concerning conservation of East Africa's wildlife was strict. She wriggled back against the hot seat and subsided, but her eyes were troubled. Somebody should report her discovery to the police.

At the crater lodge, eight thousand feet above sea level, the evening air was cool. Having showered, changed, and pulled on a heavy sweater, Kim was slumped in a chair on the terrace, looking at the remarkable view and watching the sun go down, when Neil appeared at her side, nursing a bottle of Coke.

He waved it in front of Kim's face. "Want one?"

"No, thanks."

"What's the matter with you? You're awfully glum."

"I feel glum," Kim admitted. "Neil, do you know what I saw? Down in that *manyatta?* Leopard skins piled up on the floor, two or maybe three, under a cover. I told Peter about them and he said to forget it. Why? I can't understand!"

Neil didn't answer at once. He pulled up a chair and sank into it, sighing. "Peter doesn't dare get involved," he said finally. "Look at it this way, Kim. People like you and your grandmother get down into the crater once, or at most twice. He gets down there every couple of weeks and he's got to keep on the right side of the Masai, or he'll disappoint all the clients who've been counting on seeing a *manyatta* at close hand. If the Masai suspect he's squealed on them, he won't get within a mile. Besides, what's the percentage? The police could search until doomsday and they'd never find a shred of a leopard skin."

Kim frowned. "Then all this moaning and groaning about the fate of the poor leopards is just so much talk. You watch them being killed off. You see the evidence right in front of your eyes. And you don't do a thing!"

"Don't sound so disgusted. Use your head, Kim. Picking up a couple of leopard skins from a Masai warrior isn't going to get anybody anywhere. You saw that article in the Nairobi newspaper. There's a big combine behind this poaching, and it's the top men the police want."

"Naturally. But we've got to start somewhere."

"We?" Neil raised an eyebrow and grinned.

"We who believe in the preservation of East Africa's wild animals," said Kim primly, but her eyes held a hint of mischief, and she knew she sounded as though she were quoting from a textbook.

"Oh, come off it," Neil complained.

Kim shrugged. "I've just had an idol shattered. Two idols. You and Peter."

Neil put his head against the back of the chair and let out a guffaw like a donkey's bray. "Any time I'm an idol of yours!"

"You're not, anymore. You've got feet of clay."

"Or maybe a tongue of clay. Can't you avoid the clichés?"

"I was going to tell you something else, but now maybe I won't." Kim hoped she sounded bitter.

"Don't start teasing like a ten-year-old," Neil advised, and took a leisurely sip of his Coke.

Kim let the criticism sink in, deciding she'd never confide another item of information to this patronizing Britisher. Her original impression had been the right one. With sudden total recall she could hear him speaking on the evening when they had met. Mimicking his English accent, she suggested slyly, "Perhaps you'd like to chat with my grandmother—a charming person—and you share an interest in Africa's big game. So rare in Americans."

Neil looked slightly startled, then amused. "I'll bet you're great in school plays. Kim, what more do you want to tell me? Come on, give."

The temptation was too great to resist. "Remember the man who drove up to the *manyatta* just as we left?"

"Vaguely," said Neil.

"Heavy set, thick neck, clipped hair, expensive shirt. Not an American, but maybe Yugoslav or something."

"Goodness, you should be in Scotland Yard!"

"I've seen him before," Kim confessed. "In Nairobi." She told Neil about the incident in the store. "They were trying on hats, he and this East Indian, but they were talking about something else, something that seemed very secret, in whispers."

"Women," suggested Neil with a phony leer.

Kim ignored him. "Then a man came in," she con-

97

tinued, "to pick up an order. A nice-looking young man, very outdoorsy, and when he gave his name to a clerk, the other two recognized him and snuck out of the store."

"What was the man's name, do you remember?"

Kim nodded. "I don't know why I should, but I do, because it sounded sort of romantic. John Sanderson."

Neil looked slightly more interested. "Dad knows John Sanderson pretty well. He's a game warden."

"Aha!" said Kim.

"Isn't that great! A neat little plot, wrapped up and tied with a blue ribbon."

"Stop teasing, Neil. This could be important. First I see a guy acting suspicious in Nairobi, then he appears at a Masai *manyatta*. Oh, and I forgot to tell you about last night!"

Finally Neil's interest was captured. "You're sure about the fact that there were several bills?" he asked when Kim had told her story.

"Yes, but I couldn't see how much they were worth."

"Of course not, from that distance." Neil drank the last of his Coke and put the bottle on the floor beside his chair. "It's really quite interesting. One incident, taken alone, means less than nothing. Two—not much more. But three, well it starts you speculating, doesn't it?"

Kim clasped her hands. Her eyes were sparkling. *"Now* do you think we should go to the police?"

To her disappointment, Neil shook his head. "At

this point it would get us nowhere, Kim. Consider the echelons of crime. Always there's a man at the top, whether or not he works with a gang. In the problem of collecting and disposing of loot, he's got to deal with others. He needs runners, a fence, a channel to police or political influence. He doesn't go into a big operation without some protection against discovery and prosecution."

"So?"

"So we agree he always needs somebody or something. He goes to someone he thinks he can trust, named A. This fellow A consults B, and B brings in a crony we'll call C. The echelon broadens, but only A has access to the man at the top. I think you may have run across a fellow in the C category, Kim, but I don't think he's a big shot."

Feeling a trifle deflated, Kim sat back in her chair. "What do you mean by a runner?" she asked after a while.

"A fellow who collects the loot and passes it on."

"Like leopard skins?"

"If you want to get specific. I was speaking generally."

Kim bit her lower lip, lifted the hair from the back of her neck, and thought hard. "If we could follow Mister C around, he might lead us to B and then maybe. . . ."

Neil grinned sympathetically but shook his head. "You may never see this bird again. How do you know whether he's going on into Tanzania or heading back to Kenya? Today may be the last time your paths will ever cross."

The fragrant early morning air streamed into the Land Rover as Peter drove down the curves from the rim of the crater to the great Serengeti plains. "You're in luck," he told Mrs. Gardiner. "At this time of year the savanna is usually burnt-looking and dry, but the rains have come early. Everything is green again."

The change in scenery was remarkable. The heavily forested country on the heights abruptly gave way to a flat, treeless, level plain. Ahead, the road ran straight to the horizon, then seemed to tumble off the edge of the world.

Ostriches began to come into focus, standing as high as men and stepping along on naked legs, occasionally ruffling their fanlike wings. To Kim they seemed as improbable as giraffes; it was hard to think of them as birds at all. "They look like cancan dancers," she said.

Neil agreed. "Dilapidated ones, well past their prime."

Gradually, as the miles flew under the wheels—the track here was free of potholes—zebras and wildebeests began to appear, in tens, in hundreds, and finally in thousands. Animals were grazing as far as a person could see, some no bigger than pencil dots in the distance. Kim's eyes grew tired from straining, yet she couldn't look away.

"Not thousands. There must be tens of thousands," her grandmother murmured as though she were talking to herself.

Peter nodded. "More than a million animals have been recorded in this park. Today we're seeing mostly wildebeests and zebras, but there are also more than five hundred thousand gazelles."

He pulled over to the side of the track, although there wasn't another car in sight, and cut the engine. "Look, Mrs. Gardiner! Look, Kim!" He pointed across the plain.

In the middle distance a single wildebeest had stopped grazing and started to run, seeming to roll with a rocking-chair canter into the wind. A companion followed him, then another and another, until the entire herd was on the move, traveling westward, the leaders in single file, the others following three and four abreast and forming a procession that seemed to be never-ending. As Kim watched through her binoculars, a second herd joined the first, and finally wildebeests on the move could be seen for several miles.

"It's the wrong time of year," Peter muttered. "You have no right to be seeing this! It's a migration, one of the most inspiring sights in all of East Africa."

"You can say that again," Neil said under his breath.

"Hey! That's American slang," Kim spoke to relieve the tension. Otherwise she might have burst into tears.

Nearby, the zebras were getting nervous. They lifted

their heads to the sky, neighed restlessly, then fell into line, too. Off into the distance they streamed, a painting in motion, following the lead of the wildebeests, whose beards were flying in the breeze.

Reluctantly, Peter pressed the accelerator and drove on, but the excitement of the passing scene did not lessen. On either side of the road the animals loped by, heading in the opposite direction from the Land Rover and ignoring it completely. Once in a while Kim saw the look in an animal's eyes, as though he were following, blindly but devotedly, a leader whose superior vision would take him to Elysian fields.

The tented camp at Seronera, where Kim and her grandmother would spend two nights, was ninety miles from Ngorongoro, but the drive seemed short by comparison to others they had made. As they neared the middle of the plain, strange little mountains of rock began to appear.

"Have you ever been to Morocco?" Mrs. Gardiner asked Peter. "Those rock piles remind me of the Casbahs along the road from Ouarzazate to Tenirhir."

Among flat-topped acacia trees, the towering rocks were outlined against the blue, cloud-strewn sky. To Kim, who had never seen a Casbah, they looked like abandoned fairy-tale castles.

"We call them *kopjes*," Neil said. "It's a Dutch word. I think most English and Americans refer to them as inselbergs."

Like a chain of islands or miniature oases the

kopjes led toward distant pale hills, fainter in color than the clouds. Stone piled on stone, tower on tower, they were as intricate as constructions made by an architect from a superior set of building blocks. Peter kept slowing up to inspect one after another carefully. "Ah," he said finally, and swerved off the road to get closer. "See, up there against the second stone from the top, a rock hyrax."

"A what?" Kim asked. She couldn't see a thing.

"A rock hyrax," Peter repeated. "Follow my finger. There! Along that outcropping to the left."

Fortunately the animal moved, and Kim could focus her glasses on a small, tailless creature as plump as a big brown guinea pig. "You'll see more in the rocks around our camp at Seronera," Peter said. "Sometimes you'll hear them scream in the night."

Moving on from one lodge or camp site to another at intervals of a couple of days was becoming a procedure that Kim enjoyed, because each new place was different, and she never knew what to expect. Seronera was situated in a small oasis in the middle of the plain, with several round, thatched-roof huts, a long, low dining room and kitchen built of native stone, and two rows of green canvas tents placed at right angles to one another.

She and her grandmother were assigned to a tent not far from the dining room, and as Neil helped cart their belongings from the car across the grass stubble, a small plane swooped down from the sky like an oversized bird, apparently coming in for a landing at the nearby airstrip.

Mrs. Gardiner stopped, squinted up at it, and laughed. "Somehow, airplanes look so out of place here."

Neil agreed. "Yet they're used almost as much as cars."

Kim hurried on ahead to inspect their living quarters. In front of the tent an awning was fastened to two poles, forming a kind of porch, equipped with two canvas chairs and a table holding a wash basin and pitcher. Inside were a pair of neatly made cots, a stack of towels, and a small table. Out back were primitive shower and toilet facilities. "Isn't this fun!" she cried.

"Mm-hum," replied her grandmother absently. Propped on the night table she had discovered an official-looking envelope, unsealed, which she opened while Kim stood by curiously. "Why, how nice!" Mrs. Gardiner said. "We're asked to dinner at the game warden's house. That will be very interesting."

Kim was surprised. "How come?" she asked.

"It seems the warden—his name is Bill Parson—is a close friend of Colonel Abercrombie's and he has heard I'm interested in conservation. I wonder whether there will be a party or if we'll be the only guests."

It proved to be quite a party to which Kim and her grandmother were invited. A jeep picked them up at the camp at eight o'clock, when it was already so dark they could scarcely see the Kikuyu driver. Jouncing along a track that skirted the airstrip, where two small planes were parked near a tall pole flying a wind sock, they soon came to an L-shaped building backed by two big baobab trees. In front, out from the shelter of the L, a huge log fire laid on the trampled grass was crackling away merrily, and behind it a number of dim shapes occupied a group of chairs.

Kim, following her grandmother, was introduced to one person after another. Dr. and Mrs. Clark, Major Cooksey, Mrs. Meeker, who was described as a well-known sociologist, and an English woman called Lady Clifford, whose head was wrapped in a chiffon scarf.

A boy not much older than Kim came through the dark from behind a buffet table and said, "I'm acting as bartender. What will you have to drink?"

Mrs. Gardiner asked for a gin and tonic and Kim said, "A bitter lemon would be nice."

"Now come meet the rest of our guests," suggested Mrs. Parson, a thin, quick-moving woman wearing a bush jacket. Her husband had stopped to chat with Lady Clifford and Mrs. Gardiner, who looked especially diminutive next to the game warden's six-foot-four-inch frame.

Kim followed along obediently, although she felt more comfortable tagging behind her grandmother. She was introduced to a visiting warden from another Tanzania game park, then to a tanned, curly-haired young man whom she recognized instantly—John Sanderson!

"Mr. Sanderson is also with the wildlife service, but

his home base is in Kenya," Mrs. Parson explained, as Kim shook hands with the warden whom she had first encountered in the dry-goods store in Nairobi. Something so honest and likeable about him, a warmth in his handshake and in his voice, appealed to her, and she was disappointed when Mrs. Parson whisked her away to meet still another man whose face, lit by the flickering fire, seemed vaguely familiar.

"Herr Otto von Starck," Mrs. Parson said.

"Haven't we met before?" Kim asked uncertainly.

The German, tall and impeccably groomed, bent over her hand stiffly, then inspected her with the air of a man only mildly interested in pretty girls. "It has not been my pleasure," he said.

Kim was trying to remember where she had heard that accent before as the boy who had gone for drinks came up to her with a tall glass in his hand. "I'm Pat Hulett," he said. "I'm working for Mr. Parson for a few months. Who are you?"

8

Kim snapped her fingers. "Willard's friend. Of course!"

The boy named Pat Hulett leaned closer and peered into her face in astonishment. "I beg your pardon?"

"What did you say?"

"We seem to be talking at cross purposes. I asked who you were."

"Oh! I'm sorry. I'm Catherine Kimberly, Mrs. Gardiner's granddaughter. Kim for short."

"And Willard's friend for long?"

Kim burst out laughing. She turned away from the fire and said in an undertone, "Excuse me for being so vague. I was trying to think where I'd seen Herr von Starck before. Then I suddenly remembered. It was on the roof at Treetops, more than a week ago."

"He's very handsome," Pat suggested, "but somehow I take it you were not impressed."

"Why do you say that? I've never even spoken to him—before tonight, that is." Kim studied the boy's clever face, then broke down and grinned. "What are you, a mind reader?" She took a sip of her drink and asked, waving a hand at the bowl of stars above their heads, "Do you like it here?"

"The Serengeti? I love it!" Pat replied as though he found the question rather silly. "Why, don't you?"

"I just came," Kim said. She hesitated, then added slowly, "I guess it must be wonderful really to live here. Never before in my life have I felt quite the way I did this afternoon, driving across the plains. There's such a big difference between looking at wild animals and looking at famous buildings or even famous pictures. Palaces and cathedrals can be rebuilt if they're destroyed. New pictures can be painted. But—" She stopped short. "Heavens, I've been making a speech."

"A good one," Pat said gently. "I can supply the last sentence. But once the wild animals of the Serengeti are gone, no power on earth can bring them back."

Lady Clifford strolled over, her chiffon head scarf flying. "Pat, be a dear boy and get me another drink." She held out her glass. "Isn't it nice there are two of you. Young people, I mean." She turned to Kim. "Is it very dull for you, traveling with your grandmother?"

"Dull with Grandy? Never! She's a marvelous traveling companion, and she's terribly interested in birds and wildlife and—well, everything."

"I understand she's an ardent conservationist," Lady

Clifford said to make conversation while she waited for Pat to return. "Isn't she president of New York Wildlife Preservation or something?" Then, without waiting for a reply, she asked, "Did you see the wildebeest migration this afternoon? We flew right over herd after herd on the move."

So Lady Clifford must have arrived in the little plane, Kim decided as she nodded her head. "It was marvelous!"

"Mr. Parson was just telling me a very interesting thing about wildebeests. The animals all have large lumps in their noses, and the air coming out of their lungs bounces off the lump and condenses moisture." With a nod of thanks she took the drink that Pat held out to her. "Isn't that convenient? They can survive for quite a long time without water, as a consequence."

Kim was polite, but not exactly fascinated. She glanced through the flickering firelight in the direction of Herr von Starck, and wondered how he happened to be at this party. As soon as possible she made her way across the grass to where he was standing. "I remember now where I saw you," she said. "It was on the roof at Treetops and you were talking to that American who had his passport stolen by a baboon. What was his name?"

Herr von Starck looked puzzled rather than startled. "An American? There were many Americans at Treetops when I was there, including, apparently, you and your grandmother. Isn't that true?"

Kim nodded, aware that she wasn't about to discover whether Willard's name was known to this German. "Did you see the bongo fight?" she asked to prolong the conversation.

"No. Unfortunately I slept through it."

"That's a shame. I was told it was quite an unusual occurrence."

"*Ja,* so I understand."

The interchange seemed to have reached a dead end, but Kim was persistent. "Are you on safari, like us?" she inquired.

"No, not like you."

"Oh, you're here on business, then?"

Herr von Starck smiled. "*Ja,* I am here on business. I am connected with an exporting firm in Hamburg. An acquaintance of mine sent me a letter of introduction to our host." He stopped speaking, regarded Kim intently, and seemed to be asking silently, Will that be all?

Playing dumb, Kim said, "How very pleasant." She strolled away to rejoin her grandmother, and stood listening to Mr. Parson describe the recent killing of five giraffes by Wanderobo tribesmen within the conservation area.

All of the wardens were greatly concerned about a decision by the Tanzanian government to open twenty-five hundred square miles of prime game country to agricultural development. Mr. Parson was so alarmed that he had called a meeting of Masai leaders, Nairobi newspapermen, conservationists, and representatives of the Kikuyu and Wanderobo tribes to discuss ways of blocking the move.

"What is going to happen to the wildebeest, whose ancestors have made this migration you saw starting today for thousands of years?" The question Mr. Parson asked the group gathered around him was rhetorical, but Mrs. Gardiner added another.

"If they come up against fences and Masai cattle, won't they just barge right through?"

"Nobody knows, but one thing's sure," John Sanderson said. "A lot of wild animals are going to get killed, including the last of the leopards."

"Maybe they'll retreat into the crater," suggested Mrs. Clark hopefully.

Mr. Sanderson shook his head. "Ngorongoro Crater isn't self-sufficient. The herds depend on the eastern Serengeti plains for rotational grazing and calving and on the forested highlands for water. Remember, too, that the cheetahs and leopards live on the crater walls, not down on the plain."

Major Cooksey stepped up. "Aren't you chaps getting a bit wrought up?" he asked. "I understand Canadian scientists were called in—competent fellows, I'm sure—and that they anticipate no real problem."

Herr von Starck, who had walked over to join the group, nodded affirmatively. "The press gets everybody excited, but after a while people discover things aren't so bad after all."

Mr. Parson didn't try to argue. "I wish you could see the Ivory Room at Mombasa," he said. "I wish you could see the stacks of confiscated leopard skins and the hundreds of pairs of horns taken from slaughtered rhinoceros. Then maybe you'd understand that we aren't being hysterical. The threat to the game, from poaching and from ranching, is real and imminent. There simply isn't much time left if we're going to save the Serengeti. Or perhaps I should say, if we still can."

At the long dinner table, set with a red-checked cloth and heavy country pottery, Kim found herself between Major Cooksey and John Sanderson. The major's attention was taken by Lady Clifford, on his left, so Kim welcomed a chance to get better acquainted with the attractive young Englishman from Kenya.

She learned that he was here on a special assignment. "You might call me a special investigator," he said. "We're trying to make a breakthrough on this poaching problem, but I can't say we've been very successful, so far."

Unlike Herr von Starck, he seemed to enjoy Kim's curiosity. He answered her questions gravely, treating her as an equal, not as a child, and told her that most of the wardens agreed with the press that a powerful criminal organization was supplying the black market with leopard skins and rhinoceros horns.

Kim glanced across the table, where her grandmother and Herr von Starck were chatting together. The German was undeniably handsome, and when he was talking to an older woman whom he apparently found entertaining, he lost the patronizing manner that had annoyed Kim. Grandy, on her part, seemed especially lively and showed that she was having fun. Although Kim couldn't catch a word of the conversation, she was aware that this sort of dinner party was her grandmother's mileu, that she was completely in her element.

"As I was saying," John Sanderson continued, "it's bound to be a big operation, and it isn't the Masai hunters or the other small poachers we're after. It's the men at the top."

"Still, you have to start from the bottom up, don't you?" Kim told Mr. Sanderson about seeing the stack of leopard skins, inexpertly hidden in the Ngorongoro *manyatta,* and for once she had a listener who accorded her story the seriousness she felt it deserved.

"The trouble is, by the time I could get there, even if you'd been able to talk to me earlier, the skins would have been spirited away. Leopards? Not a Masai in the place would admit to having seen a leopard on the crater walls in years, let alone kill one for its hide."

Mr. Sanderson's remarks led Kim to describe the earlier experience, when she and Neil had come across the beautiful leopard in the tree near Amboseli and had seen its subsequent tragic fate. "Have you ever felt," she asked, "that you're right on the edge of something important, that if you could only fit a lot of bits and pieces together you could come up with some valuable information?"

"Are you still talking about poaching?"

Kim nodded. "I know it sounds silly, because here I am just a girl on safari with her grandmother, but people I've seen or talked to keep showing up again in peculiar situations." She told him about the man with the wart on his nose who had left the Nairobi store in a hurry right after the warden himself had entered, and about the dark-skinned driver to whom this same heavy-set man had given money the night before he showed up at the *manyatta*. "There are too many coincidences," she said with a shake of her head.

Mr. Sanderson was inclined to agree. "Here," he said, taking out a business card and writing his telephone number on it. "Keep your eyes open, Kim. They're sharp eyes and they see things. In fact, just because you're so young and unlikely to arouse suspicion, you might turn up something Bill Parson and the rest of us would never have a crack at. If anything else happens—anything that seems at all fishy—give me a ring, and reverse the charges. Phone any time," he added, "day or night."

"Eggy scram or eggy fry?" asked the waiter assigned to the table where Kim was breakfasting.

"One scrambled egg, please," she answered automatically. She wasn't thinking about food, but about last night's supper party, and the game wardens' concern for the animals.

"*Chai?* Coffee?"

"*Chai.*" Usually Kim preferred milk to tea, but the morning was so cool she craved something hot.

Her grandmother had breakfasted earlier, but Kim had gone straight from the dawn game run to the one-room museum, where Neil had wanted to show her the poachers' equipment.

On display were spears, wire traps, snares, and poisoned arrows taken from captured tribesmen. Neil took an oval noose, held open by thin, plaited vegetable fibres, down from a hook on the wall. "It's easy to fasten this along a game path at the right height to catch the head of an animal. Knot the other end of the wire around a nearby sapling and you have a good primitive trap."

Kim shuddered, because she could see the picture. The more frantically the animal struggled, the faster he would be choked to death. She turned away to inspect the stuffed birds in the little museum's collection, but the memory of the murderous equipment remained with her.

As she sat and sipped the hot tea, she made notes on a scratch pad. Peebee would have her term paper, an essay full of eyewitness news. Kim was glad she had decided to write about poaching, and in particular about leopard poaching. If only she could do something important to help instead of just reporting.

At the far end of the room the headwaiter and an assistant were setting up a long table laid with a linen cloth and napkins and decorated with centerpieces of fresh flowers into which were stuck a dozen small Tanzanian flags.

"Looks as though you were having a special party," Kim said as she left the dining room.

The headwaiter nodded. "Mr. Parson is holding a luncheon meeting. We're trying to do something a little special, because he says some important people will be here."

The important people, Kim discovered later, were a very odd lot. Among them was an incredibly tall Masai warrior in ochre paint and typical battle costume who towered over even Mr. Parson. "Look, Grandy, isn't that the Masai chief from Ngorongoro?" she whispered as they passed him outside the small bar.

Mrs. Gardiner nodded. "It is indeed."

"He must be a really big shot."

"I wouldn't be surprised." Mrs. Gardiner was as fascinated as Kim by the collection of characters assembling in the dining room. The chief approached the flower-decked table, which was surrounded by a buzz of flies. Following him was a shorter, dark-complexioned, somewhat beaky man, evidently also a person of authority, who wore a long, heavy army overcoat clutched over his bare chest and an ancient top hat, which he kept on his head even when he was seated. John Sanderson and the Tanzanian game wardens Kim had met the previous evening entered together. They were accompanied by a bespectacled Kikuyu in black trousers and a white shirt, whose ambulatory note-taking indicated that he must be a newspaper reporter. Mr. Parson escorted two latecomers, probably Kikuyu and Wanderobo tribesmen, according to Neil. The contrast in costumes was so remarkable that Kim couldn't stifle a laugh. "They look as though they were going to a Halloween party," she said.

Mr. Sanderson had the privilege of sitting next to the Masai, and the idea occurred to Kim to send her new friend a short note. "The Masai is headman at that *manyatta* in the crater," she wrote on a slip of paper, and sent it over to him by a waiter, hoping she wasn't being too brash.

That afternoon it rained hard, and Kim huddled in the tent with her grandmother, swatting mosquitoes as she ruminated on her term paper, for which last evening's various conversations had given her several new ideas.

She recounted in detail her talk with John Sanderson, and brought Grandy up-to-date on her encounter with the scar-cheeked bus driver and her suspicions concerning the man with the wart on his nose, reviewing the three encounters in which he had figured. "I like Mr. Sanderson," she paused to confess. "He doesn't treat me like a crazy kid."

"You're far from a crazy kid, Kim. But to some older

people you probably seem very intense—perhaps a little too curious."

"I know. Herr von Starck couldn't get away from me fast enough, but he seemed to take a terrific shine to you."

"Nonsense," Grandy protested. "But I must say he's perfectly fascinating. A real German aristocrat, with the most polished manners."

"Which he doesn't waste on a teen-ager," Kim said with a grin.

At this point Peter came by to say that the sky was clearing. "It will be muddy going, I'm afraid, but even so we may have a decent game run," he called through the closed flap.

Kim was more than ready to leave the dripping tent. "Come on, Grandy. Let's go!"

Mrs. Gardiner yawned. "You go. I think I'll read. It's awfully wet outside."

"It's awfully wet in here," countered Kim as she pulled on her safari boots. "Besides, sure as fate, if you don't come along you'll be sorry. Suppose you miss a leopard or something really great?"

It wasn't a leopard they saw that afternoon, but something equally spectacular. At sunset, after Peter had skidded the Land Rover through a hundred soggy puddles, he suddenly cut the motor and pointed toward the glistening savanna off to the left. There, on a slope, were three cheetahs out hunting, walking casually through the shoulder-high grass with their aristocratic heads alert. They made an unforgettable

118

picture, which no camera could ever quite capture, because the animals were so sleek and voluptuous. The light through which they moved was as chimerical as a dream, at one moment saffron, at another gray or pink.

Kim and her grandmother, Peter and Neil all stood on the car seats, crowded into the open hatch, quietly watching the cheetahs until they disappeared.

"Somebody said that a cheetah looks like a greyhound dressed in a leopard skin," said Mrs. Gardiner as they drove back. "I used to think that was amusing, but now I know that person had never seen a cheetah in the wild."

At camp, all traces of the game wardens and the tribesmen had disappeared, nor did Kim see either Mr. Parson or John Sanderson again. Peter suggested an early start the next morning for Keekoruk Lodge in the Masai-Mara Reserve, so Kim and her grandmother went to bed at nine o'clock, as exhausted as children by all the intensive looking they had done in the late afternoon. The twelve hours of darkness and twelve of light shortened the evenings and seemed to make such early retiring natural, although many of the other campers were still strolling back to their tents as Kim tried to go to sleep.

In the African stillness voices carried clearly. "Much as they do in the Arctic," Grandy remarked. The anguished barks of baboons and the wailing of hyenas mingled with an occasional laugh, or a remark caught out of context and therefore intriguing.

". . . don't be silly, all these drivers get rich on tips."

"And so, this is their country, not ours."

". . . a beautiful guy, a really beautiful guy."

The cheetah, Kim thought sleepily. She must be talking about the cheetah. . . . A really beautiful guy.

Kim drifted off as the camp settled down, despite the occasional roar of a lion or the hyenas' perpetual crying of the blues. Stars twinkled above the trees. The dying moon drifted downward. Then, without any warning, a scream split the air, bolting Kim upright on her cot. Piercing, raucous, loud as a train whistle, it rose to a terrifying crescendo. "Good grief, what's that?" Kim whispered, certain that a wild beast must be lurking right outside the tent flap.

"I don't know." Grandy started to giggle nervously.

"Could it be a lion?"

"Lions don't scream, darling."

"An orangutan?"

"You're on the wrong continent, silly girl."

Again the silent night was ripped apart by the siren-like wail, now coming from immediately overhead.

"Go to sleep," Kim heard a man in the next tent advise his companion. "It's only a tree hyrax."

"I don't believe it," Kim muttered as she snuggled under the covers once more. "You can't tell me a little animal the size of a bunny rabbit could ever make a noise like that!"

120

9

Peter drove back into Kenya for a stopover of a day and a night at Keekerok Lodge, where game was plentiful. Kim counted nineteen lions, eighty-one elephants, thirty-seven giraffes, and an undetermined number of baby hyenas playing outside the entrance to their burrow.

In the afternoon, while her grandmother napped, she changed to a swimsuit and lay in a long chair beside a small, icy swimming pool, soaking up the sun. She had been there for barely half an hour when she raised her head to see Neil, in swimming trunks, crossing the lawn with a disjointed lope that reminded her of a giraffe. Raising her hand, Kim signaled. "Coming for a swim?"

"In just a few minutes." Neil had brought some bread from the dining room to feed to the dozens of vervet monkeys squabbling and playing in the tall trees bordering the lawn.

Kim propped herself on her elbows and watched him, a familiar figure now, tanned and freckled on his face, neck, and lower arms but milk-white where a shirt usually covered his body. A cockscomb of bleached hair straggled over his forehead, and he looked utterly absorbed in his attempts to coax the skittish monkeys to eat out of his hand.

Dear Neil, Kim thought. He was far from handsome, no prince on a white charger, but he had a sense of humor and was basically a good guy. How often her initial impression had been wrong, and later she became fond of a person who had antagonized her on first meeting.

After scattering the last crumbs on the ground, Neil came over and joined her, easing his length to a duck-covered mattress on the pool's concrete deck. "This is the life," he said. "Utter luxury after our leaky tents."

"I rather liked the tents," Kim confessed, "except for the hyrax, if it was a hyrax." She told him about her terror in the night.

Neil laughed. "Peter should have warned you. They're screechy little beasts." He added, "We've seen the last of them, now that we're back in Kenya. You can take comfort in that."

He put his head down and closed his eyes, but after a few minutes Kim roused him. "Neil?"

"Umh?"

"Remember, yesterday at lunch, when I sent that note to Mr. Sanderson?"

"Uh-huh."

"Do you think the Masai chief noticed?"

"Uh-huh."

"Neil, wake up! Did you hear what I asked?"

Neil raised his head. "Yes, and the answer is still yes. He was aware of the note and also he was aware of the glance you and Mr. Sanderson exchanged as we all came into the dining room. I'm the observant type."

"Are you teasing or are you serious?" Kim asked.

"I'm quite serious, and since we're asking questions, what was the note all about?"

"Oh, I just told him that the Masai chief's *manyatta* was where I saw the leopard skins."

"Well, goody," muttered Neil. "So now the chief knows that Mr. Sanderson knows everything that you know. The Masai may be primitive, but they're not dumb, lovey. Couldn't you have picked a better time to get in touch?"

Kim shook her head. Somehow, on this golden afternoon, the problems of the game wardens and the wildlife enthusiasts seemed remote. "I may never see him again," she said.

"Hey!" Neil objected to the note of regret in her voice. "Sanderson's old enough to be your father."

"He is not. I'll bet he's not much over thirty," Kim retorted, but she flushed, nevertheless.

"Thirty's positively ancient. You stick to somebody in your own age group. Now listen to Uncle Neil!"

"Uncle Neil!" Kim scoffed. "When you're just two years older than I am."

"OK, then. Stick to me."

The next day, on the endless drive along the eastern wall of the great Rift valley and straight through Nairobi to Tsavo West National Park, sixty miles on the other side of the city, they continued their teasing, but there was no bite to it. Neil is getting positively affectionate, Kim thought without dismay.

Dusty, dead tired, and stiff from jouncing in the back of the Land Rover, Kim finally climbed down from the car before the door of a lodge called Kilaguni, where the rooms had angled balconies overlooking a water hole a few hundred yards away.

By the time she and her grandmother were settled, it was dusk, and elephants were coming to the nearby salt lick, while herds of impalas and Thompson's gazelles moved through the shadows on the other side of the pond.

"It's all perfectly beautiful," Grandy yawned, "but I'm almost too tired to care. Let's have an early supper, get to bed, and start living again tomorrow. What do you say?"

Kim was agreeable, so her grandmother went one step further. "Let's not even change."

"You mean eat in our safari clothes?"

"Why not? Other people do when they get in late."

"Grandy, you're slipping!"

"Let's say I've slipped," Mrs. Gardiner proposed. She linked her arm through her granddaughter's and led her toward the door.

Just before noon, the next day, Kim was crossing the parking area in front of the lodge when a Zebra Tours bus came lurching into the turnaround and pulled up almost in front of her.

From the front seat descended a familiar figure carrying a flower-decorated straw bag. "Mopsy!" Kim groaned to herself, but when Mrs. Collins turned and spotted her, she was pleasant and even cordial. "Well," she said brightly to her grandmother's friend, "our paths cross again."

Mrs. Collins wiped her perspiring face with a clean handkerchief. "For the last time, I'm afraid. Tomorrow is the windup of our tour, although a few of my traveling companions are going on to Mombasa."

"And you're going back home?"

As she spoke Kim was looking over Mrs. Collins's shoulder at the driver, who was helping some of the other passengers to alight. A sharp-chinned African with a long welt on his right cheek. . . . She recognized him instantly.

"Yes, and I can't say I'm sorry, although I must admit the trip was very interesting. Still, I'm not accustomed to quite such long hours."

Kim was scarcely listening. "You've changed drivers," she said.

"Oh, yes. The other man got sick—stomach trouble or something. Where's your grandmother?" Mrs. Collins asked.

This time Kim didn't even hear the question, because she was watching the last of the passengers descend from the bus. Second from the end came Willard, disguised to some extent by purple sunglasses, but perfectly recognizable.

Mrs. Collins turned too. "Who's so interesting?"

"That man in the dark glasses. Has he always been with your tour?"

"Oh, no. He just joined up with us yesterday. It seems his wife's ill in a Nairobi hospital—she has hepatitis or something—and he's just putting in time until she gets well enough to travel again."

A likely story, Kim thought, although she had no real reason to feel doubtful. "How well do you know him, Mrs. Collins?" she asked.

"Oh, not well at all." Mopsy started to giggle and lowered her voice to a whisper. "You might say we're traveling acquaintances rather than traveling companions. I've never met a man so terrified of women. He seems absolutely lost without his wife. Did you say your grandmother was asleep?"

"No. She's in our room writing letters. I'll tell her you're here," Kim promised. Then, remembering her manners, she said, "That bag looks heavy. Let me carry it into the lobby for you."

Mrs. Collins relinquished her burden gratefully, and toddled along beside Kim on swollen feet. The rest of the passengers had dashed inside hurriedly, acting like a bunch of vacationists tumbling over one another in their anxiety to board an airplane and get the best seats. Among them was Mr. Vernon W. Bixel, chewing on the remnants of a cigar. He had changed his sports coat for a brand-new safari jacket and some equally new trousers and boots. To Kim he seemed out of character, all gussied up, from the bald patch gleaming on the top of his head to the binoculars hanging from his arm. When she passed close to him she instinctively wrinkled her nose, because he reeked of toilet water, still pungent even after the morning's drive. If Willard recognized her—which he surely must, Kim thought, toting up the number of times he had been within eyeshot of her fairly unusual red hair —he gave no sign. Absorbed with his billfold and his passport, he shouldered his way determinedly into the throng around the desk.

"Oh, dear!" Mrs. Collins exclaimed. "I seem to have left my gloves on the front seat of the bus. Kim, be a darling and run get them for me, will you?" She looked down at her bulging ankles. "I don't think I can walk another step."

Kim was glad to oblige and went off to the zebra-striped bus. There were the white cotton gloves, looking out of place on an African safari, but the bus was locked up tight and the driver had disappeared.

"Oh, my, you couldn't find them?"

Kim did wish that Mopsy would stop prefixing every remark, important or trivial, with *oh*. "The bus is locked," she explained, "but they're right where you left them. We can get them later, any time the driver is around."

Actually, she would enjoy a casual brush with that driver, Kim was thinking. Today, instead of finding Mrs. Collins a burden, she was anxious to see more of her, because she was her chief contact with two characters who interested her very much, the dark-skinned driver and the American leopard-skin hunter who had mislaid his wife. She was not disturbed in the least when Mopsy suggested, *sotto voce,* "Tell your grandmother I'm here and that I suggest we lunch together. I don't have to eat every meal with the Zebras, and besides I have something very mysterious I want to tell her about."

Mopsy's last remark was enough to whet Kim's ever-ready curiosity and send her plunging into the bedroom. "Your fat friend's here and we're going to have lunch with her," she announced.

"Sh! Kim! Don't be rude! She could be in the next room." Mrs. Gardiner put down her pen and asked thoughtfully, "What about Peter and Neil? Mopsy will bore them stiff."

"I've called them off," Kim told her grandmother. "They'll lunch alone. They understand."

"Well, I must say *I* don't understand." Mrs. Gardiner ran her fingers through her unruly hair and leaned against the back of the chair. "What makes you so enthusiastic about my old schoolmate all of a sudden? Is Mopsy wearing a stolen leopard skin?"

Kim burst out laughing, because the image was so nonsensical. "No, but she has something very mysterious she wants to tell you about."

"Mysterious? Mopsy?"

"Yes, and it isn't about Mr. McGregor's garden." Kim was still laughing. "She's traveling on the bus with that driver I was telling you about, the one who took some money from the man with the wart on his nose. And guess who else? Mr. Vernon W. Bixel, Willard for short."

Mrs. Gardiner didn't sound astonished or even especially interested. "Is she?" she murmured and turned to the envelope she was addressing. "What time does she want us to lunch?"

At Kilaguni the open-air dining room was a vast, raised terrace, bordered on the side facing the water hole by a low stone wall, and roofed by a rough wooden frame in which birds nested, flying back and forth at will or perching on chair backs to scan the floor for crumbs.

Mrs. Collins was already ensconced at a table close to the parapet—and consequently the view—when Kim and her grandmother arrived. She beckoned to them with a raised plump arm and a welcoming smile on her freshly powdered face. "Right over here, dears!"

"Well, Mopsy," said Mrs. Gardiner as soon as she was seated, "Kim tells me you've had a good trip."

"But tiring, very tiring. The jolting in that bus, even though I'm sitting up next to the driver!" Mrs. Collins dropped her voice to a whisper. "The best seat," she explained confidentially.

"And you've seen lots of animals?"

"Enough to last me a lifetime, and not all of the sights were pleasant. We saw a dead hippopotamus yesterday, floating upside down in a pool, while a whole crowd of lions waited for him to drift ashore. The hippo was all bloated and blown up, like a big rubber toy, and our guide said the lions were going to eat that thing. Ugh!" Mopsy wrinkled her short pink nose in disgust, but the experience didn't seem to affect her appetite.

Lunch, as usual, was a buffet, with cold meat and salads, sliced chicken, and hot dishes set out on a long table. A waiter took orders for tea or coffee, but the guests picked up plates and helped themselves.

Once the three of them were settled again at the table, Kim decided it was time to bring up the one subject she might find really interesting. "You said you had something very mysterious to tell Grandy, Mrs. Collins."

"I do indeed." While Kim stopped eating and looked hopeful, Mopsy sawed away at a piece of meat and said, "This beef is tough."

"The meats aren't very good," Mrs. Gardiner agreed, "but the salads are so delicious I can make a meal on those."

130

"Not I," replied Mrs. Collins firmly. "I always say a meal without meat isn't worth eating. Rabbit food has never been my dish."

Kim could scarcely stifle a giggle. She looked down at her plate and avoided her grandmother's eye. With a nickname like Mopsy and a figure to match, could anyone fail to see the humor in a remark like that?

The waiter came with coffee, another distraction that contributed to Kim's growing impatience. How could she get the conversation back on the track? If she came out with another reminder to Mrs. Collins, her grandmother would surely consider her rude.

Fortunately Grandy herself took the plunge. "I'm all ears to hear about your mysterious happening," she said.

Mopsy leaned forward conspiratorially and pitched her voice to a sibilant hiss. "Well, you see it was this way. It may not mean anything but then again it may, and it might even be worthwhile to watch the Nairobi papers and see if there has been a robbery." The idea apparently just had occurred to her. "You know, it might." She speared another piece of the beef and chewed away thoughtfully while Kim squirmed.

"A robbery?" Mrs. Gardiner prodded.

"I'm not saying it was or it wasn't, Ellen. I'm just saying it looked peculiar, extremely peculiar, to me."

"What looked peculiar, Mopsy?"

"I was just going to tell you, but I'd better begin at the beginning. You see, what with the way my legs swell up and everything—it's an ailment I've had ever since I was your age," she said in an aside to Kim. "Anyway, the other members of the group very kindly let me ride up front."

"How convenient for you," murmured Mrs. Gardiner.

"Well, I don't know, it's still not all that comfortable. And the dust! The dust is perfectly awful. The driver can't seem to remember to wind up his window when we pass another car. Anyway, yesterday the dust seemed particularly dreadful, and I got this terrible coughing fit. Really terrible. Actually, Ellen, I could scarcely get my breath."

"Tsk, tsk," clucked Mrs. Gardiner, while Kim stifled a sigh.

Mopsy, abandoning the beef, tackled a piece of chicken and stopped talking to ruminate. Kim passed the sugar to her grandmother and managed a surreptitious wink. Mrs. Gardiner looked unnaturally sober, as though she was determined to keep her face straight. She measured a scant half teaspoon of sugar and let the grains fall slowly into her black coffee, avoiding Kim's eye.

"Now, let's see, where was I."

"You were choking," Kim blurted out.

"Oh, yes. Nothing seemed to help. Nothing! That nice Mrs. Winquist who sits behind me kept slapping me on the back, but it didn't do a bit of good. I was positively crying. I was really scared!"

132

"Of course you were," murmured Mrs. Gardiner sympathetically.

"The driver was new—maybe Kim told you," continued Mopsy. "I don't like him as much as the other one, but perhaps it's because he's got such a bad scar on his cheek, the cheek facing my direction in the bus, I mean."

"More coffee, madam?" asked the waiter, arriving with a steaming pot in his hand.

"Yes, thank you," said Mrs. Gardiner.

"I'm not drinking coffee," said Kim.

"No, thank you," said Mrs. Collins. "Now I've lost track again. Oh, yes. I was telling you about the driver. Even he got worried about me, and finally he said, 'Would you like a cough drop?' and I nodded. You see, I wasn't even able to talk."

Kim and Mrs. Gardiner both wagged their heads.

"Anyway, he stopped the bus and took the keys out of the ignition and opened the glove compartment and got me a box of Smith Brothers cough drops. Imagine finding those all the way over here in East Africa!"

"Is that the mystery?" Kim asked.

"Of course not, dear. It's what I saw when the driver opened the glove compartment." Once more Mrs. Collins's voice dropped to a whisper. "You understand my eyes were all but shut. I was really having a paroxysm of coughing. But even so, even though the glove compartment was open for only a split second and then, pop, closed up tight again, guess what I saw?"

"What?" asked Kim and her grandmother in unison.

"A big wad of bills!"

"Is that the mystery?" Kim realized she was repeating herself.

"The mystery," said Mrs. Collins, her eyes round, "is where any bus driver could come by that much cash. There weren't just a few bills, you understand. It was an enormous roll of money, held by a rubber band, literally hundreds of dollars—shillings, I mean. Now what do you make of that?"

Mrs. Gardiner had no quick answer, but she did have a piece of advice. "It looks as though your driver has a very profitable sideline, and it's also fairly obvious he's the type who gets into fights. If I were you, I'd stay out of the whole thing, Mopsy. You're starting home tomorrow. Just forget what you saw."

"Oh, I hadn't planned to go to the police or anything, but it *is* mysterious, and rather frightening, don't you agree?"

Mrs. Gardiner nodded, but Kim thought *mysterious* was not quite the word. Undoubtedly the driver was up to something shady, and she suspected he could be a swag man for native poachers. How could she find out?

10

Kim was still pondering this question as she nibbled at a piece of fruit while the two older women were finishing dessert. "Did you ever get your gloves, Mrs. Collins?" she asked. Then she suggested, "I could go see if the bus is unlocked now."

"You stay out of this, too!" Mrs. Gardiner ordered her grandchild. However, Kim had already pushed back her chair, excused herself, and was leaving the dining room.

Neil was lounging in the lobby, waiting for her, and together the two walked to the main entrance and peered out at the buses and safari cars baking in the sun of early afternoon. Kim didn't explain her errand, but simply stood and ran her eye over the drivers, some of whom slept in the open cars, while others crouched in a ring under the branches of a spreading acacia tree.

"What are they doing?" she asked Neil.

"Playing Weso. It's a strange game, very complicated, yet it's popular all over Africa. Let's go over and have a look."

"Should we?" Kim was hesitant, although she was in no special hurry to return to the dining room either with or without the gloves.

"Sure. The men all love kibitzers. It makes the game more exciting."

Kim followed Neil across the hard-packed earth and peered over the heads of the nearest players. In the center of the group was a rough wooden board in which four rows of cup-shaped hollows had been scooped out. Two of the drivers were moving pebbles quickly from one hollow to the next and then to the next. Every once in a while one or the other picked up a handful of pebbles from one of the cups—apparently without any reason—and put them on the ground at his feet. Meanwhile, the spectators kept talking excitedly, and even though she couldn't understand a word, Kim could tell that they were making comments on the play and suggesting moves to the opponents. Everybody wanted to get in on the act.

Neil stood with his hands thrust into his pockets, a slight smile on his face, his eyes following the play, but Kim soon grew restless. She glanced back to where the Zebra bus was parked just in time to see the scarfaced driver slam the front door and start across the grass to join the fun.

He squatted along with the rest, his back to the

parked cars, and at once became deeply involved in the game, offering opinions and shouting advice along with the other spectators.

Kim seized the opportunity to slip away from the group. "Stay here," she whispered to Neil. "I'll be right back." Then she strolled over in a desultory manner to where the zebra-striped Volkswagen was parked.

The windows had been opened, evidently to lower the inside temperature, and the doors left unlocked, since the driver was more or less on guard. The white gloves were still there, crushed against the back of the right-hand front seat. Kim needed only to reach in and pick them up.

Before doing so, however, she glanced hastily around at the Weso players. The scene had not changed. The men were still absorbed. Opening the bus door, Kim climbed partially inside, and reached out to punch the latch of the glove compartment, although she had little hope that it, too, would be unlocked.

To her surprise the door fell forward, but the compartment was quite empty, except for a scrap of crumpled paper and an opened package of Smith Brothers cough lozenges. Mopsy's "enormous roll of bills" was not there. Because the paper, a sheet torn from a note pad, had some writing on it, Kim took it out to examine more closely. At that point, however, a whistle sounded behind her, and she slammed the glove compartment shut and quickly picked up the gloves.

"Anything you want in there, miss?" the scar-faced

driver asked. His whistle had been peremptory, and his face was scowling.

"Yes, but I found them, thank you." Kim managed a smile, which she hoped looked innocent. "Mrs. Collins's gloves."

Since they were in her hand, this sounded logical enough, but Kim was afraid that the click of the glove compartment latch had been audible. Also, she was especially aware of the crumpled paper she had palmed and wouldn't have been surprised in the least if the driver had investigated further; but a burst of laughter from the crowd surrounding the Weso players caught his attention. With a nod and a grunt, he hurried back to the game.

Kim didn't return to the group, as she had promised Neil. She took the gloves to Mrs. Collins, who was sitting on the terrace still chatting with Grandy, then went straight to her room where she smoothed out the slip of paper on the dresser top, hoping it might give her a clue as to where the money had come from. Or, for that matter, where it had now gone.

The penciled scrawl was not immediately decipherable, because the light in the room was dim after the brilliant sun. Kim took off her sunglasses, squinted experimentally at the script, then carried the paper out to the balcony. Down at the water hole a single rhinoceros, motionless as a stone sphinx, was braving the afternoon heat.

Kim dropped into a deck chair. Ah, this was better. The paper contained some kind of list. "Mombasa

27," she read. "Ind ex," then "Mahdi," and underneath on a slant, "Lamu 19."

Disappointed, although she knew that to turn up a real clue would have been a very long shot indeed, Kim tucked the note in her pants' pocket and resolved to show it to Neil. If he agreed it was nothing but gobbledegook, she'd simply throw it away. At that moment there was a knock on the door and Kim went over to admit her grandmother. "I escaped," she said thankfully. "My goodness, people of one's own generation can grow tedious. Kim, I recommend that you start right now breaking old school ties."

She kicked off her shoes and lay flat on the bed. "Call me ten minutes before it's time to leave for the afternoon game run," she suggested. "That is, if I should fall asleep."

Two minutes later, as her grandmother started to snore gently—Grandy had the most ladylike snore Kim had ever heard!—another soft knock came at the door. This time it was Neil, and Kim slipped out and joined him. "Where can we be alone?" she asked at once.

"Ah, sweet child, come with me to the Casbah!" Neil dropped his voice to a low rumble and held out his arms.

"Don't be an idiot. I've got something I want to show you in private, and there isn't much privacy around here."

"You're so right," Neil agreed. "Shall we take a walk around the compound?"

Kim shook her head. "It's too hot."

"Let's try a corner of the lounge. It's almost deserted at this time of day."

Indeed, the place was empty except for a white-haired old gentleman, dozing with his head on his chest, and a thin woman with glasses, writing letters. Kim led the way to a pair of high-backed chairs and pulled them close to the parapet, then showed Neil the crumpled paper she had taken from the Volkswagon, reading it over his shoulder:

Mombasa 27
Ind ex
Mahdi
Lamu 19

"Do you think it means anything or is it just gibberish?" she asked.

Neil studied the note for a minute before replying. "It may not mean anything to us, but it must make sense to somebody. Looks like a man's writing."

"I suppose so. Women are usually more fussy about the way they form their letters," Kim agreed.

"Let's really study this," Neil proposed. "Mombasa, of course, is the big port city of Kenya, as you'll see in a very few days now." He glanced across at Kim briefly, telling her without words that he was sorry to see the safari drawing to an end. "The number 27 could be anything. A date, a person's age, a street number."

"If it's a date," said Kim, "and it refers to February,

Grandy and I will be there. It's the day before we fly home."

"You'll also be on Lamu," Neil reminded her. Arrangements had been made for Peter to drive his clients to Mombasa, stay with them for a day of sightseeing, then say good-bye at the Mombasa airport on February 24, where a small chartered plane would fly them to the island of Lamu for a couple of days of ocean swimming and rest. Returning to Mombasa on the twenty-sixth, Kim and her grandmother would spend one more night at the Oceanic Hotel, then leave by air early on the following day for Nairobi and their Pan Am jet connection.

"If 19 is a date, too, and we're talking in the same terms, it's too late," Kim said. "Today's the nineteenth." Then she asked, "What do you think Ind ex means?"

Neil shook his head. "I haven't the foggiest."

"Mahdi." Kim's eye had traveled on downward. "That's a funny word. Could it be the name of an African tribe?"

Neil shook his head again. "No tribe I've ever heard of. As a matter of fact, I don't think it's an African word at all. It sounds more like Arabic to me."

"Arabic?"

"Pity we don't have an Arabic dictionary. We could look it up." Shrugging, Neil added, "I have one at home, but no matter. There are plenty of Arabs in Mombasa. When we get there we can find out if I'm right."

Kim sighed. She hated waiting for things. If only they could decode this strange message straight off! "At least Lamu means something," she said as Neil handed back the piece of paper. "Or it will when we get there. Hey! Didn't Grandy say that Lamu is an old Arab settlement? Maybe that's the connection. Mahdi —Lamu 19."

Neil, tired of trying to solve the puzzle, leaned back in the chair. "I envy you, going to Lamu," he said.

"I wish you were coming along." Kim meant this sincerely. She would miss Neil and Peter, miss their spirited descriptions of the tribes through whose lands they had passed, miss their quickness in spotting birds and knowing their names—marvelous names like long-tailed widow bird, golden pipit, lily hopper, lilac-breasted roller, superb starling. She liked the superb starlings best of all, with their metallic blue backs and scarlet breasts, and their improbable name. Next she liked the golden pipit. "When he flying is looking yellow like butterfly," she had heard a Kikuyu driver say.

Kim roused from her reverie and heard Neil answer, "I wish I were, too." He was looking at her almost tenderly. "It's been fun knowing you."

"There's no need to put things in the past tense yet." Kim stood up. "I'll see you at four. Or did Peter say four thirty?"

The afternoon game run was disappointing. Animals were scarce, although Peter did manage to find several dik-diks and some small herds of impalas and hartebeests. The Zebra Tours people were luckier. They came back to the lodge with tales of a big herd of elephants and two lions off by themselves on a honeymoon.

Kim took the opportunity to approach Mr. Bixel. "Good evening," she said with a smile. "Isn't it interesting the way our paths keep crossing?"

"They do?"

"Don't you remember me?" Kim asked.

"Can't say I do." Willard looked at her red hair as though it were apt to catch fire. He edged away.

"Now, Mr. Bixel!" Kim played coy. "I'm offended, really I am. The first time we saw each other was back in Nairobi, when you were trying to buy a leopard skin for your playroom. Then I returned your passport to you at Treetops, after that scamp of a baboon stole it. You can't have forgotten that?"

Willard swallowed hard. Snapping his fingers, he said, "Sure, now I remember," but he looked around apprehensively, as though he wouldn't want to be overheard.

"Where are you headed now?" Kim was persistent, although she felt her smile was beginning to jell.

"Me? I'm with Zebra Tours."

"Oh, then you go back to Nairobi tomorrow morning?"

Willard nodded absently, but a tour member standing to his left said, "Not this guy. He's headed for Mombasa, the lucky stiff."

Kim spread her hands and appealed to Mr. Bixel. "Which is it?"

"Mombasa," he admitted reluctantly. Either he was very nervous or very stupid, Kim decided. The outstanding trait he had exhibited in the past, however, was cupidity. There was also the possibility that he was lying. She decided to try to keep him on the hook.

"I've always wondered about that leopard skin. Did you finally buy it?" Kim hoped she looked and sounded more ingenuous than she felt.

"No, not that one." Willard took out a fresh cigar, put it in his mouth without lighting it, and started to move away.

"Well, who knows, we may meet again," Kim called after him, but she felt the conversation had been less than profitable. She hadn't unearthed a thing she didn't already know, except that Mr. Vernon W. Bixel was headed for Mombasa, a fact he seemed curiously reluctant to admit.

That night, propped up in bed and surrounded by her grandmother's conservation journals, Kim was making notes for her term paper without quite the enthusiasm the subject deserved.

Her mind kept straying from the data she was accumulating on the poaching problem to the sort of personalities that must be involved, and from there to the real people she had brushed up against on this safari who had one thing in common: they were acting unexpectedly.

Flipping the pages of the notebook until she found a clean sheet, Kim started to make a sort of list-outline, lettered according to Neil's method, A, B, C, D.

Beside the letter D she wrote: "Masai and other tribal poachers."

Beside C: "Runners like the scar-faced driver, who may be passing out cash in receipt for leopard skins or rhino horns."

At B she hesitated, then wrote: "What about the thick-necked Yugoslav with the wart on his nose? Is he B or C? He doesn't want to be seen with an Indian in Nairobi. He has money dealings with Scar-Face. He showed up at the *manyatta,* but nothing really *proves* he's interested in leopard skins."

Next to A, reserved for the man at the top, Kim wrote absolutely nothing, although she chewed her pencil abstractedly and found herself thinking about Vernon W. Bixel.

She had no reason to suspect him, really. No reason at all. Except that while he seemed stupid, he might be very devious, a clever actor who pretended to be something he was not. The first time she had seen him with his long-suffering wife in the Indian export shop in Nairobi, he had appeared to be merely obnoxious. At Treetops he had stayed in character, a pushy American trying to drum up an acquaintanceship with the handsome but aloof Herr von Starck. Then today. To-day Kim couldn't explain, unless he had considered her assumed coyness a threat. The notion made her smile, because for a girl her age to be interested in a man like Willard was inconceivable!

All things considered, however, Vernon W. Bixel of the many visas was not a good candidate for position A in this hierarchy of criminals Kim was dreaming up. Yet she didn't like the man, and, furthermore, she mistrusted her own assessment of his character.

"Good night, sweetie." Grandy closed her book and reached up to turn off the reading light. "Don't work too late. We have to get an early start tomorrow."

"I'll stop right now." Kim gathered up the magazines and stacked them beside the bed. "Tomorrow it's a tented camp again, isn't it? Beside a river. That should be different, and fun." As she lay awake in the dark, she resolved to stop trying to disentangle the threads of a mystery that trained investigators like John Sanderson were finding insoluble, and spend the remaining time simply enjoying herself!

John Sanderson made her think of Neil and his quick reaction—jealousy?—to her interest in the older man. Neil brought Kim's thoughts around to Peter, and his reluctance to become involved in anything to do with Masai misbehavior. Yet she remembered the grim look on his face when he had discovered the skinned leopard. Peter was a noncombatant sympathizer, she decided. He was on the side of the goodies but, figuratively speaking, he refused to carry a gun.

146

11

The green tents of Tsavo Tsafaris stretched in a straight row fifty yards beyond the far bank of a fast-flowing river, which Kim and her grandmother had to cross in a precariously small rubber boat, rowed by a grinning African who kept assuring them in broken English that it would be quite safe.

Peter and Neil, waiting to come along on the second trip, echoed this reassurance, and stood waving as the tubby little craft swung into the current, apparently highly amused at the expression of alarm on Mrs. Gardiner's face.

Upstream from the camp the country was hilly, and the water rushed downward in search of its channel, uncovering layers of rock lying close to the surface of the rapidly sloping bed. It creamed over flat stones like cooking caramel and gushed onward, making the crossing tricky but not impossible.

On the opposite shore, a hundred yards downstream from where the boatman had pushed off, the game warden, who doubled as camp manager, sauntered across the grass to greet the new arrivals. He was accompanied by a boy to cart the luggage and a tall, ungainly ostrich, who stepped along fastidiously and peered inquisitively at Kim's red hair.

Sparsely feathered and awkward, the bird reminded her of a boy who has suddenly outgrown his clothes. When she climbed out of the boat, he followed her up the bank and stood blinking down at her from a great height. "Goodness," she murmured, unconsciously mimicking one of Grandy's expressions, "is he tame?"

The camp manager nodded. "He's been raised right here in camp." Slapping the creature familiarly on the rump, he said, "Buzz off, Ossie. You're nothing but a big, bumbling teen-ager." To Kim and her grandmother he explained, "He'll be prettier later when he gets a full complement of feathers. Ossie is just six months old."

Even so, Kim realized that the ostrich had almost attained his full growth. Standing nearly seven feet tall, he followed along after the porter in a friendly fashion, stepping high and putting his two-toed feet down with a precise, mincing gait.

Ossie was not the only tame bird on the place. There were a pair of beautiful Egyptian geese and a handsome peacock, who sauntered back and forth in front of the row of tents, spreading his tail at intervals and stopping to be admired. Grandy got out her camera and obligingly took his picture, while Kim tossed her safari jacket on one of the cots and went off to explore. This string of tents was situated in the largest game park in the world, eight thousand square miles of bush on either side of the Nairobi-Mombasa road. Great herds of elephants roamed these hills, along with buffaloes, rhinoceros, and all manner of antelope, including the fringe-eared oryx and the lesser kudu, with spiral horns and white-striped coat. A group of tourists who had just returned from a morning game run were exultant because they had seen a pair of kudus. Clustered under the spreading branches of a baobab tree, a trio of ardent photographers were relaxing in canvas chairs and congratulating one another on their great good luck. Kim wandered past them and went back to the boat landing, where Peter and Neil had finally arrived and were lifting their duffel bags ashore.

"So you made it!" Kim called down to them, grinning. "I never expected to see you again."

"Oh, we're tough characters," Peter replied jovially. "Though there was a point when I thought we might be swept right on to Malindi, and leave you and your grandmother to follow along behind with the car."

"Does this river go all the way to Malindi?" Kim asked curiously.

Peter nodded, laughing. " 'Even the weariest river winds somewhere safe to sea' " he quoted, "and this river is far from weary. The rains have given it a new lease on life."

Kim gazed down at the rushing muddy water.

"What's it called—the Athi?" She was trying to remember the notation on the itinerary.

Peter shook his head. "This is the Galana, but you're almost right. The Athi flows into it." He swung his bag over his shoulder and started off, whistling, to find his tent.

Neil seemed in no hurry to get settled. He loitered on the riverbank with Kim, savoring the wildness of the camp's location, and telling her that here she would probably see the largest herds of elephants they had yet encountered on the trip. "The camp keeps a couple of trucks on this side of the river," he said, "and there's a fairly decent system of roads through the bush, or so I understand from Peter. I've never been here before myself."

"Who drives—Peter?" Kim inquired.

"No, a ranger. For once Peter goes along for the ride. Get him to tell you some of his elephant stories. He used to hunt them, you know, in Uganda."

Kim hadn't known. "Kill them, you mean?"

Neil nodded. "Under government supervision, of course. There are parts of the country in which elephants multiply so rapidly there's a real population problem."

Kim was relieved to discuss some animal other than the leopard. As she had promised herself the night before, she was doing her best to put the poaching mystery out of her mind and enjoy the scene at hand. During lunch, served under the trees near the river's edge, she questioned Peter about his Uganda adventure, but found him reluctant to talk about shooting in any form.

"It was necessary," he said, "but it wasn't pleasant. You see, I have a great admiration for elephants. They're among the most intelligent creatures on earth."

"Just before we left home I read a very interesting article in *Holiday* magazine," Mrs. Gardiner said, leaning forward. "It seems that at Voi—that's right near here, isn't it?—there has been a lot of poaching."

Kim groaned inwardly. Poaching again! She couldn't seem to escape the subject.

Peter, meanwhile, was nodding his head. "The natives shoot the elephants with poisoned arrows, and sometimes a poor beast runs for miles before he drops, while the poachers watch for circling vultures to spot their kill." He turned to Kim. "Of course, as you know, they're after the ivory."

"Anyway," Mrs. Gardiner broke in, "the game warden at Voi somehow claims that other members of the herd often stay with a wounded elephant until he dies. Then they pull out his tusks with their trunks and hide them in the jungle."

Peter leaned back in his chair and laughed. "That's a pretty tall story," he said. "Elephants are bright, that's certain, but I can't believe they're clever enough to try to frustrate the poachers, and what other explanation for such conduct could there be?"

The afternoon drifted by. Kim read in the shade of

the tent's awning until it was time for the game run. Then she and her grandmother climbed to wooden seats in a high-bodied, open-sided truck, along with Neil, Peter, and a young couple who admitted happily that they were spending their honeymoon on safari in Africa.

A hilly, rock-strewn track wove in and out through dense scrub until, after more than an hour, the driver pulled up before an enormous, flat-topped stone as big as a small hill. Everyone was allowed to get out and scale the smooth sides of Mudanda Rock, set in a natural amphitheater.

Neil's prediction that Kim would see more elephants here than ever before came true. Hundreds of animals browsed in the bush near a water hole on the far side of the great rock, chewing away complacently on the ample vegetation and paying not the slightest attention to the spectators crouching or standing on the rocky bleachers above.

"A full grown bull can eat half a ton of food a day." Peter, always full of interesting facts about the wildlife encountered, added to this statistic by saying that elephants also needed a great deal of water, at least fifty gallons between dawn and dark. This explained why such vast herds stayed close to the Galano; they had no need to travel far with such an ample river nearby.

From the Mudanda Rock the truck swung around in a semicircle, heading home along the broad stream, which even down here maintained a swift flow. On the opposite bank trees were stripped bare of leaves, and the bark of many of the trunks had been rubbed away by elephants scratching their backs to rid themselves of ticks or flies. Red stained the bare trees as well as the animals themselves, the red of the river mud and the savanna clay. Every few minutes the driver would stop to point out still another herd on the opposite bank, bulls and cows and big babies moving along with slow precision, completely unconcerned by the rackety motor of the laboring truck.

It was dark when Kim and her grandmother, stiff from the long drive, went to their tent to wash up for dinner. Without changing from their safari clothes, they got out flashlights and found their way to the lean-to where the evening meal was being served.

After dinner Mrs. Gardiner went back to the tent, while Peter joined the game warden in the open-air bar. Kim and Neil, well-fed but not in the least sleepy, stretched out in the canvas chairs under the baobab tree and looked out at the rushing river and up through the branches at the moonlit sky.

Lizards rustled in the leaves over their heads, cicadas sang in the grass, and in the distance an elephant trumpeted. "It's all very African, isn't it?" Kim observed as she glanced along the line of tents faced by trees and bushes, which took on fantastic and rather eerie shapes in the light of the oil lanterns that hung from each canopy.

Neil nodded. "This camp seems more remote than

the others, probably because our car is parked across the river, and there's no way of getting in and out except by boat."

"That boat!"

"I understand there's usually an outboard motor," Neil said, sounding slightly defensive. "The chap who brought us across says it's away being repaired." He had taken out his pocket flashlight and was playing with it. "Let's walk down to the landing," he proposed. "Sometimes, on a moonlit night like this, elephants come down to the water to drink. We might be lucky." He held out his hand. "Come on!"

There was no dock, but the rubber boat had been pulled up the steep bank to rest on the spreading roots of a flame tree, which leaned out over the water. The oars, worn from repeated scraping against stones and totally devoid of paint, rested against the tree trunk. From here the lantern lights glimmered faintly, and the moon suddenly attained a new dimension, lighting the sky and the swirling water with an unearthly glow.

Kim sank down on the pillowy edge of the inflated boat, and Neil sprawled on the coarse grass beside her, leaning on his elbow and peering across the river toward the opposite bank. "The wind's right," he murmured. "Our scent is blowing back toward camp. Let's keep very quiet for a while."

Kim nodded agreement. She had no need to talk, but her racing thoughts had returned to the leopard poachers. All of the experiences she had reported to

John Sanderson now seemed almost impossible, the safari was nearly over, and she was probably destined to leave East Africa not one bit wiser than she was tonight.

Suddenly Neil touched her knee. "Look!" he whispered, pointing.

Kim peered through the stream of moonlight coming over her shoulders toward a clump of thornbush and a huge dark boulder on the opposite bank. Then she heard a strange sound, like an enormous stomach rumbling, and slowly the boulder began to move.

Down the sloping bank toward the water it came, a mud-stained colossus gradually identifiable as an elephant with huge flanks and flapping ears. Swaying in the slow rhythm with which elephants usually move, the great beast ploughed through the mud at the water's edge, then stood stock-still, his ears no longer flapping, but fanned out. He didn't lower his trunk to drink. He simply stood and looked, once more immobile as a rock, but alert.

"What's he looking at?" Kim whispered, her mouth close to Neil's ear. "Us?"

Neil shook his head and put a finger to his lips, while Kim returned to her contemplation of the elephant, a one-tusker, who continued to hold his motionless pose as the red water swirled around his feet. Then she was aware of another noise, a scraping sound accompanied by water slapping. Neil pulled her down to the ground beside him, and she wriggled around to lie on her stomach, craning her neck to get a better view upstream.

Riding the rapids above the camp was a crude but strong dugout, with an oarsman fore and aft, pinned for a moment in the moon's path; then it disappeared as it swung toward shore and under the arching trees. Kim could hear the grunt of the hollowed log as it scraped the stones of the riverbed, and the protest of the oarsman in the stern as he tried to get his craft back into the current. Again the dugout emerged into the moonlight, and now Kim could see that it was filled with some sort of cargo, packages wrapped in dark coverings and tied with heavy twine.

Still the elephant didn't move. Blending with the rusty water and the red earth of the bank, he was almost invisible. In any event, Kim's attention was now centered on the boat and its occupants, two dark-skinned young men stripped to the waist, struggling to keep the dugout on course through the rapids.

The task was impossible. The rushing water caught the stern and swung the dugout about like a child's toy, first toward one bank, then the other. The rowers were skillful, but the swollen river fought back. Kim caught her breath, expecting, in each successive second, that the boat would overturn.

The narrow craft was rushing in the camp's direction, the stem cutting the swirling water, the man in the bow pulling his dripping blade from the oarlock to push at the root-netted bank. He was within a few feet of Kim and Neil now, directly in the moon's beam. With a grimace that exposed a bright gold tooth, he gave a mighty shove, and the boat spun around, to be caught up in a whirlpool, which headed it unexpectedly toward the opposite bank.

Kim clutched Neil's arm. "The elephant!" she gasped. About to scramble to her feet to call out a warning, she felt a firm grasp on her wrist.

"Keep still!" Neil commanded in an undertone.

Kim bit her lip, uncertain whether to obey her natural impulse or the authority in Neil's voice. Then she gasped again, as she watched the stricken boat hurtle to the very feet of the shadowy five-ton animal.

Now, at last, the one-tusker raised his trunk and screamed. The sound was dreadful, a shriek that rent the night and made Kim shudder with terror. The elephant took a step forward toward the heavily laden dugout, and before the men could pole out of harm's way, he lowered his powerful trunk.

Kim covered her eyes with her hands, but peered through the cracks between her fingers, every nerve tense. A bull elephant like this could pick up a man like a doll, toss him into the brush, and pound him to quick death with his massive feet. But the animal bypassed the dark form in the bow and instead lifted a square package from behind the forward strut, brought it up to his mouth, and ripped at the covering in an obvious attempt to discover whether the contents were edible.

With a frenzied cry that sounded more animal than human, the man in the bow pushed against the stones along the bank, and the dugout once more was caught up by the swift current. It came racing past Kim and Neil, on a straight course at last, and entered the calmer waters below the camp on its reckless run to the sea.

Meanwhile the elephant flapped his big ears like sails and angrily flicked his short tail over his rump. Apparently the package contained no foodstuff to his liking. With an impatient swing of his trunk, which he used like a hand, he flung his trophy into the middle of the river. Then he lowered his trunk to do what he had come for—drink.

Kim's and Neil's attention was now riveted on the package being jounced from stone to stone along the rapids, catching here or there for a second, then swirling on even faster than the dugout disappearing downstream. Now it was opposite them, less than a boat length away, where it was picked up and tossed on, then battered against a succession of rocks, and finally caught by its cord on a stubby branch emerging from a half-submerged log.

"We can get it!" Kim breathed.

Neil was not quite so sanguine. "How?"

"In the rubber boat, silly. It's only a few feet from shore."

But those few feet were dangerous, as they both knew. One false move, and they would be unable to row against the current, even though the rapids were well above the spot where the package had lodged.

"How good a rower are you?" Kim remembered to ask.

"Fair," said Neil modestly. Then he sat up. "Look, the elephant has gone."

Kim glanced across the river. Indeed, the huge pachyderm had disappeared into the bush so silently that she began to wonder if he'd been there at all. But the cargo caught on the log was evidence, and she knew that Neil shared her curiosity to see what was in it.

Scrambling to her feet, she helped lift the rubber boat and slide it into the water, then edged back up the slippery bank to hand Neil the oars.

"You're not coming!"

"Oh, yes I am," Kim replied, and before a serious argument could start, she leaped into the tubby craft and pushed off.

"If your grandmother ever finds out—"

"Oh, Neil, don't be idiotic. Grandy would be just as anxious as we are to capture that cargo." She clung to the sides of the boat and watched the muscles on Neil's arms tense as he plied the oars.

Within minutes it became obvious that they'd never make it. The boat was too light to pit against the strong current. Neil poled it back to shore. Together they pulled it slowly upstream by its painter, and worked their way back to a spot above the landing where they could make a second try.

They stumbled along in the shadows of the big trees, trying to make as little noise as possible, and hoping they wouldn't be detected by Peter or the game warden, who surely would put an end to their dangerous game. All the familiar night sounds smote their ears—the staccato call of a jackal, the dismal *whoo-oo, whoo-oo* of hyenas, the cough of a startled impala, which caught a glimpse of them from the water's edge, then bounded off in sure-footed high leaps, heading upstream.

Kim skidded into the water, soaking her safari boots, as she helped launch the rubber boat once more. This time Neil considered his strategy more carefully. "You sit in the bow," he said, "and try to grab the package as we go past. I won't be able to hold steady for more than a second, and then only if we're lucky. We'll head downstream a-kiting and come in just about where we did before."

Kim saluted. "Aye, aye, sir." She scrambled over and knelt as close to the inflated edge of the bow as she dared, knowing that Neil was right. She'd have to be quick and hope that she could unsnag the cord before their prize was whirled away.

"And for Pete's sake, don't fall overboard," Neil warned.

Kim didn't deign to reply. She was too busy planning her own campaign. If she lay quite flat on her stomach, with only her arms and shoulders above the rim of the boat, she should be secure enough, yet free to rip the cord from the stub on which it had caught.

"Now!" Neil called before she was quite ready. Leaning forward, Kim gave a vicious twitch to the hemp tying the water-soaked bundle, which was wrapped in a slippery oiled cloth. The stubby branch held, and so did the wet cord, but the jerk was enough to free the package itself. As the boat headed uncontrollably downstream once more, Kim and Neil watched the wrapping slowly pull away, revealing in the moonlight its contents—a magnificent, tawny leopard skin, which rushed on downstream as though it were alive.

12

"Neil! Do something!" Kim cried.

"If that isn't just like a woman! What do you expect me to do, jump in and swim after it?" Neil was having his own troubles, trying to keep the rubber boat from being swept out into the current. He needed every bit of strength he possessed to inch it back to shore.

In seconds the leopard skin was out of sight, careering down the swift-flowing river to be snared in a thicket of clinging brush or caught on a jagged rock, or, water-soaked at last, sink to the bottom. "Such a waste, such a waste," Kim murmured. She wasn't thinking of the thousand dollars the hide might have brought in a Nairobi shop but of the magnificent animal who once had worn the splendid coat. "We've got to phone John Sanderson right away," she added as Neil finally nudged the boat ashore.

"Are you kidding? There's no telephone booth here, or haven't you noticed? We're in the wilderness."

"You mean now that we've got some real evidence, we're just going to have to sit and do nothing?" Kim was aghast at such bad luck.

"Nothing until tomorrow morning, anyway. There's a petrol station near the main gate. We can phone from there."

"And meanwhile the criminals escape?"

"Possibly, but only possibly. They won't reach Malindi, no matter how fast they travel, in less than twelve hours."

This information relieved Kim somewhat. If John Sanderson could alert the police and the boat could be intercepted when it reached the coast, time might still be in their favor.

"Kim?"

"Yes?"

"You didn't recognize that fellow in the bow, did you?"

"No. Did you?"

Neil nodded. "It was the guy I was talking to at the *manyatta* in Ngorongoro Crater, while you were barging about inside. I was almost sure when I first saw him. Then that gold tooth shining in the moonlight was a dead giveaway."

Kim was crawling out of the boat cautiously, trying to find footing in the least muddy spot on the bank. "All the way down here? Are you sure, Neil?"

"I could practically swear to it." He tried to haul the boat up to its original resting place, but he needed Kim's help. Together they pulled and tugged, then sank down on the dry grass breathlessly.

"Maybe it *is* one big combine," Kim suggested as she stripped off her soaked boots and poured the water out of them. "Maybe it all ties in, after all."

"It figures," Neil agreed, "but we're still on the lowest echelon of the ladder. You start with the native poachers and then you have to work your way up."

"What do you mean *you?*" Kim complained. "It's the Kenya police who are going to have to work their way up, not me!" She added as an afterthought, "I'm going back to school in a few more days."

She rose, picked up her shoes, and trudged across the prickly grass in her socks, heading toward the tent where her grandmother was already asleep. Neil ambled along solicitously, said a whispered good-night, and then turned back to the quarters he shared with Peter. Kim undressed in the dark and slipped into bed.

The next morning, awakened at sunrise by a kitchen helper bringing a pitcher of hot water and a pot of tea, Kim told her grandmother about the astonishing incident with the elephant, the poachers, and the leopard skin. She also told her about the promise she had made to John Sanderson, back in the Serengeti. "We ought to reach him as soon as possible. Don't you agree?"

Grandy nodded decisively. "Let's pack and get out of here," she said at once. "Thank goodness we have our own car!"

The river, however, was still between four people and a quick takeoff. Again the rubber boat had to make two trips, and time slipped by at an alarming rate of speed. When Peter finally turned into the twenty-mile track leading to the game park's gate, it was well after nine o'clock. Kim kept checking her wristwatch and wishing she had the wings of a fish eagle poised nearby on the top branch of a dead tree. If only she could fly!

Tommies bounded across the road, and a pair of grazing giraffes stretched their long necks and peered after the plume of dust which followed the car. But today, for the first time, not even Peter remarked on the game. Alerted to the importance of reaching a telephone as quickly as possible, he was as anxious as Kim to make time.

Everybody conjectured on the speed the poachers could make downriver. Peter figured it would take fourteen hours, rather than twelve, and even more if a portage or two were necessary. Neil bemoaned the fact that they had been unable to retrieve the leopard skin and bring it along as concrete evidence, but Kim put her faith firmly in John Sanderson. He had believed her initial report. He had asked her to phone. He would be able to act the minute he got the news.

At the gate they encountered an unforeseen delay.

The keeper, a sleepy-eyed Kikuyu, dragged his feet and spent a good fifteen minutes poring over Peter's credentials. Then he insisted on examining the passports of the Americans, which had to be unearthed from their luggage, and asked Neil a dozen pointless questions in Swahili before he would let the party through.

Peter was furious and Grandy was fuming, while Kim could feel her heart racing with impatience. But nothing could hurry the guard, who had his own conception of his duties and couldn't know that while he detained these innocent travelers others who were not so innocent might make an escape.

Finally he lifted the restraining bar and Peter stepped on the gas. With a squeal of tires, a gratifying backfire, and a cloud of dust, which enveloped the Kikuyu and finally blotted him from sight, they were off.

"Maybe you'd better do the phoning, Peter. Or you, Grandy." At the last moment Kim turned young and nervous.

"Nonsense. Mr. Sanderson asked you to call, not one of us."

Neil sat silent, evidently feeling left out. Kim noticed that whenever John Sanderson's name came into the conversation he seemed to retreat.

At exactly ten o'clock the Land Rover stopped before the forward tank in the big, modern gas station beside the Mombasa road. While Peter gassed up and

166

checked the oil and water, Kim went inside and struggled with the telephone. She had John Sanderson's card, with his telephone number on it, firmly clutched in her hand, but she couldn't cope with the Swahili coming across the line.

Frantic, she rushed for the door. "Neil! Come help me!"

Then she ran back to the phone and cried, "Just a minute, just a minute. Don't hang up," forgetting that the operator couldn't understand a word.

Neil, quite obviously, relished his role as rescuer. He was almost maddeningly calm, demanding an English-speaking operator to whom he imparted the number, then handing the receiver back to Kim with a rather superior smile.

Kim mumbled her thanks and hung on, while unfamiliar clicks and whines were finally succeeded by a comforting long-drawn-out ring. "Ah!" Kim breathed.

Her relief was short-lived. The first ring was succeeded by another, then by a third and fourth. "Sorry, madam, there is no answer," a very British voice finally said.

"No answer?" Kim hadn't envisioned this contingency. Frustrated, biting her lip in discouragement, she made her way back to the car.

With every passing mile the road to Mombasa seemed longer, although posts marked with the abbreviation *Msa* were proof that the kilometers were gradually slipping away. As the Land Rover dropped down toward the coast, the temperature rose, until by noon it reached a hundred degrees. Kim, using a series of tissues, sat mopping her face and fretting. "Could we stop somewhere soon and try again?" she begged.

Peter was both willing and anxious, but telephones were scarce, even along this macadamized road, the best the country afforded. He stopped three times, once at a dingy little restaurant where the phone was out of order, and twice at filling stations where the attendants shook their heads at his inquiry.

"Do you want to break the trip for lunch somewhere, or would you prefer to drive on?" Peter asked Mrs. Gardiner after the last negative reply.

"Oh, let's go on, if you don't mind," she replied unhesitatingly. "I understand there's a pool at the hotel, and at this point a swim sounds far more interesting than lunch."

Again they drove downhill to the salt flats and the outskirts of the city, where roadside stands, heaped with fruit and vegetables, buzzed with flies, and women in bright Katanga cottons bargained endlessly or laughed and talked in groups. Trucks rumbled along the road, school children straggled homeward, and housewives wielded homemade brooms on the hard-packed earth before their peeling stucco houses. Everything looked incredibly drab.

Kim, on the back seat, thought wearily that the safari was over. Whatever happened now, even getting through to John Sanderson, was bound to be an anticlimax. Like Grandy, she could scarcely wait to get into that pool!

At the hotel a swim, a sandwich, and a glass of iced tea revived her, and once more she tried to reach Mr. Sanderson from the bedroom telephone. By contrast to the tented camp the Oceanic, a high-rise hotel with balconies facing the sea, seemed luxurious, but contemporary comfort did not extend to the telephone system. To get a call through to Nairobi was no easier here than in the petrol station on the Mombasa road. Now the lines were busy.

Meanwhile, Kim discussed with her grandmother the thought that they might tell their story to the city police.

As she stood in front of the mirror brushing her short hair, Mrs. Gardiner considered the suggestion. "I don't think they'd take us seriously, Kim. I think it would be a waste of time."

"Perhaps if Peter—"

The telephone bell made Kim start, and she turned hopefully to answer it, but the caller was only Neil, phoning from downstairs. "How soon can you be ready? Peter's waiting outside with the car and we've got an appointment with Mr. de Souza, who'll show us through the Ivory Room. Officially, it's closed to visitors after twelve noon, so we're very lucky!"

169

"Just a minute." Kim turned to her grandmother. "It's Neil. Do you want to see the Ivory Room?"

"Of course I do! Mr. Parson was very firm about my not missing it." She put down her brush. "Tell him we'll be right down."

The sun was on the wane by now, but the city sidewalks retained their heat until twilight. Mvita Road, a dusty, deserted street in a poor section of town, looked far from exciting, although a barred door flanked by a small guardhouse indicated that beyond the locked grillwork lay the captured treasure trove both Kim and her grandmother were so anxious to see.

Mr. de Souza, a dignified, serious Indian in Western dress, represented the game department. Assisted by a couple of guards and an African helper, he apparently took charge of the confiscated loot that lined the walls.

To Mrs. Gardiner he was unfailingly polite. Kim and Neil he virtually ignored, and Peter's presence he took for granted. They had obviously met under similar circumstances before.

After the blazing sunlight the huge room seemed unnaturally dark to Kim. She wrinkled her nose at the smell of disinfectant, but was eager to hear every informative word that passed Mr. de Souza's lips.

Shelf after shelf was filled with numbered pairs of rhino horns, poachers' loot confiscated by the police and held there for government auction. "Five hundred

170

white rhinos and a hundred black rhinos were killed by poachers to get this cache," he said. "No wonder the white rhino is nearly extinct in Kenya." He shook his head in discouragement. "Seven thousand pounds of horn," he added.

"What will you do with it all?" Mrs. Gardiner asked.

"Auction it off. We hold an auction here every six months. It will bring about fifteen dollars a pound, if the market isn't deflated by too much being sold at once."

"Why would people want it?" Kim asked curiously. "Where does it go?"

"To Hong Kong, to Aden, to India," Mr. de Souza replied sadly. "It's used for knife handles, ground up for an aphrodisiac, carved into ornaments." As he talked he moved on to the next rack. "Hippo teeth," he said, "worth about two dollars a pound, and ivory. We haven't many elephant tusks here at the moment, but we have a good many animal hides."

He led them over to a pile of skins lying on the floor in a corner. "For an eland like this a poacher gets only about ten shillings," he said. "The Masai are usually responsible for the buffalo and leopard hides. You may have heard that there are more leopard skins imported to Kenya than exported. It's true."

"I don't understand," said Grandy.

"The poachers get the hides out of Kenya, often on coastal dhows," Mr. de Souza replied patiently. "Then

171

they're shipped back in legally. They aren't even cured until they get back here, because a raw leopard skin can enter the country as a hide, but a cured one is liable to seventy-five percent duty."

Kim wanted to ask how the poachers who had handled all this deplorable stuff had been apprehended, but it was difficult to interrupt. "How do you catch the poachers?" she broke in when he finally paused for breath.

"Through informers, usually. You see—" and he was off again on a different subject, describing the woolly bear caterpillar that commonly attacked the uncured skins, and for which the disagreeable disinfectant was a deterrent. Meanwhile he continued to circumnavigate the room.

Informers, Kim was thinking. The four of them could turn informers, if only Mr. de Souza would listen, instead of talking. But at that moment he glanced at the wall clock and said abruptly, "I am very sorry, but you will have to excuse me. I have a very important appointment at precisely five o'clock."

"Who do informers inform?" Kim asked a trifle wildly as the Indian shook her hand.

"The police, my dear child. Naturally, the police. That is not our department. We merely take care of the material we are sent."

So another opportunity was lost, and Kim's frustration mounted. On the back seat of the Land Rover she sat pouting beside Neil as Peter drove down to the Old Harbor past Fort Jesus, a sixteenth-century Portuguese castle, weathered and immense, then through the Old Town, where narrow streets were shadowed by high houses with ornamental balconies, and itinerant Arabs sold coffee from long-beaked copper pots.

Beneath the balconies were shops from which Oriental music drifted, and on the streets were Swahilis in long white robes, Moslem women draped from head to toe in black *buibuis,* and Hindus who brushed against Arabs in beaded hats. The town had less bustle than in Nairobi, but even more color. Peter took his time along Mbarak Hinawi Road, then pulled up at the edge of an embankment and pointed offshore at a cluster of high brown boats with furled sails.

"These are the coastal dhows Mr. de Souza was talking about," he said. "Once a friend of mine traveled to Zanzibar on one. He arrived quite safely, except that the rats ate his shoes while he was asleep."

Kim shuddered at the thought, but the boats interested her. They reminded her of the Chinese junks she had seen in pictures, uniformly dun-colored and mysterious. The vessels bore strange, unpronounceable names, and Kim could imagine the cargo—finely woven carpets and Arab chests, coffee and contraband.

Into the harbor, its lateen sails highlighted by the setting sun, slipped another dhow to join the half dozen or so already anchored. It came in close to the dock, then swung broadside to the watching group

173

as the anchor was dropped. Kim spelled out the name painted in fading letters up near the bow.

"*M-a-h-d-i.* Mahdi!" she cried, and clutched the arm of the person nearest her, who happened to be Neil. "Mahdi! Remember? On the slip of paper I found in the Volkswagon bus!"

Almost jumping up and down in excitement, she rooted through her wallet to find the carefully preserved scrap discovered in the glove compartment, then passed it triumphantly around. "See, there's the word, and this is the ship, so the list must mean something. Something important. Oh, Grandy, let's hurry back to the hotel. We've got to reach Mr. Sanderson, because now we've got even more to tell him than before!"

"Will you place your call later, please?" the operator suggested. "The lines to Nairobi are all busy."

Mrs. Gardiner, now almost as impatient as Kim, fumed at the delay. For an hour, as they bathed and dressed for dinner, the two had spelled each other at the telephone, intermittently discussing the strange message in which they had finally found a clue to one word.

"Could something be hidden in the index of a book?" Kim wondered aloud. "If 27 and 19 are dates, what could the dates mean?" Slipping her feet into yellow slippers, which matched the color of her dress, she stood staring at the grubby scrap of paper that had caused all the excitement.

174

Mombasa 27
Ind ex
Mahdi
Lamu 19

The list of words could have been in code, so undecipherable did the complete message seem.

"We should be going downstairs," Grandy said, turning from the recalcitrant telephone. She smoothed the skirt of her white dress and glanced in the mirror to check her appearance.

"You look lovely," Kim assured her. "You've got a terrific tan, and it's marvelous against white."

Mrs. Gardiner acknowledged the compliment gracefully. "Though I must say I haven't much interest in my appearance this evening," she confessed. "It seems the wrong time for a farewell party, somehow. I wish Peter and Neil were going on with us to Lamu."

The die was cast, however. Tonight, on their last evening together, the four would dine in the hotel as Mrs. Gardiner's guests, but tomorrow morning, at the airport, they would part.

There were flowers on the table, and a French wine had been ordered, but Kim found that even the novelty of a dance floor and orchestra failed to make her feel festive. She kept glancing at Neil and forcing herself to realize that, in all likelihood, their paths would never cross again.

"Dance?" he asked unexpectedly as the soup course was cleared.

Kim was so startled she stood up at once. She had never envisioned Neil on a dance floor, but he proved to have a smooth sense of timing and an authority to which Kim's feet responded. When they returned to the table, they both felt more relaxed.

Before dessert and coffee Kim excused herself and went out to the lobby telephone, but although the lines had been cleared, there was still no answer at John Sanderson's number. In despair, she sat down at a desk and scribbled a hasty note, outlining her discoveries and mentioning the date on which she and her grandmother expected to return from Lamu —February 26. "We'll be at the Oceanic for one last night," she wrote. "Then we're flying home."

Once the letter was mailed she felt better, and could "join the party," as Peter put it teasingly. "It's nice to have you with us," he added. "Quite frankly, I've missed you, Kim."

Warmed by the unaccustomed banter, Kim glanced from one to another of her companions. The professional hunter and the tall boy from Nairobi were strangers no longer, but friends. For Grandy, whom she had always enjoyed, Kim had acquired a new respect. She was a great traveling companion, who had bridged the generation gap by her gaiety and her interest in every new experience.

That interest was conspicuous the next morning at the airport, where a bright red Cessna chartered for them by Colonel Abercrombie waited to fly the two Americans to Lamu.

Kim was feeling depressed, because the safari seemed somehow unfinished. "Try Mr. Sanderson again by telephone," she begged Neil. "And this afternoon, when you get back to Nairobi, go straight to his office, please!"

Neil promised that he'd do everything possible. "Dad may have an angle," he suggested. "As soon as I get home I'll give him a rundown on the whole bit and maybe he'll know the proper person to contact if Sanderson still hasn't shown up."

"Write me at the Oceanic, tonight!" Kim demanded. "I'll be dying of curiosity. Mark the letter 'Hold for arrival' so I'll be sure to get it when we come back on the twenty-sixth."

Even though the luggage was stowed away, and the pilot was ready to leave, Kim still hung back, feeling that the ascent of the plane would tear her away from the final pages of a story she longed to finish. She shook hands solemnly with both Peter and Neil, and reluctantly climbed to the wing and then inside.

"*Kwaheri!*" Peter called.

"Good-bye!" Neil echoed. "Take care!"

Kim waved from behind the plane's window, trying to smile and conquer her sense of frustration, but her eyes filled with tears. Her grandmother, however, was settling down happily. "Isn't this going to be fun?" she shouted above the engine's roar.

13

The air route to the Arab island of Lamu skirted the coast north of Mombasa, past curving beaches protected by an almost continuous reef. Small fishing boats dotted the aquamarine water, and a road snaked from one coastal village to another. Inland there was nothing but jungle, inhabited, according to the pilot, by vast herds of elephants.

Kim leaned forward and called, "Tell us when we get to Malindi, will you, please?" Her thoughts were skipping back to the dugout and the poachers. They might even now be unloading their illicit cargo at some sheltered spot near the place where the Galana River emptied into the sea.

Ten minutes later the pilot dipped his left wing. "Down there," he said, "where the break in the reef lets the rollers come in."

Kim craned her neck, but Malindi would always remain a blur in her mind, a cluster of pastel buildings along a curving bay. She saw what appeared to be a number of inlets, but even though the plane was flying low, any river emerging from the jungle was hidden by a dense stand of trees.

Kim settled back with a sigh and tried to follow her grandmother's example and look ahead, not back. Lamu 19, she decided, was worth keeping very much in mind. Though now it seemed to mean as little as Mahdi had meant only yesterday, luck might conceivably still be on her side, and any chance for a new breakthrough should not be ignored.

The road below dwindled to a dry weather track, then became a flooded morass, and the wildness of the country increased. The plane was heading northeast now, and in less than half an hour the pilot eased down to buzz a low-lying white building facing the beach, settled in a cluster of small cottages like a hen among her brood.

"Lamu," the pilot said, pointing out a toy village a few miles farther on.

"Does Lamu 19 mean anything to you?" Kim roused herself to inquire.

"Nineteen's my birthday, that's all."

The little Cessna made a short and bumpy landing on a mown field on the mainland. "Sorry," the pilot apologized. "The wild pigs keep digging holes in the runway. It makes for a rocky ride."

A trio of teen-age boys was on hand to meet the plane. Even before the propeller stopped turning, they loped across the field to collect the luggage the pilot handed out, making off with it along a narrow path through the woods.

"Goodness, where are they going?" Grandy asked.

"To the boat landing. It's about half a mile away," the pilot explained. "Just follow along after them. The hotel launch will be coming to pick you up. You probably noticed that I signaled as we went past."

"You'll come back for us the day after tomorrow, at the same time?" For once, Kim felt, Grandy sounded apprehensive, and no wonder! Seemingly they had reached the last outpost of civilization, the very end of the world at the edge of the Indian Ocean.

"Don't worry, I'll be here, give or take ten minutes from nine o'clock." The pilot shook hands and climbed back into the cockpit, where he started the motor, while his clients trudged bravely after their suitcases, balanced on the shoulders of the three young boys.

Mosquitoes made the half-mile walk pure torture, but at last Kim and her grandmother emerged from the mangrove-bordered path to a long concrete jetty, at the end of which a substantial-looking white launch waited. Across the bay lay the town of Lamu, looking more like a toy village than ever. It was hard to believe that this collection of painted houses had a history dating back to the beginning of the Christian era, but the guidebook stated that Lamu had been mentioned in a Greek sailors' manual written no later than 110 A.D.

"Lamu is supposed to be the most truly Arab town on the East African coast," Kim's grandmother remarked happily. "And think of the invaders it has survived! Somalis, Portuguese, cannibals, the British. Do you know that Rider Haggard's brother was once a vice-consul in Lamu?"

Kim was quite used to her grandmother's quick digressions, but she had to confess that Rider Haggard was an unfamiliar name. "In his day he was a very famous writer," her grandmother assured her. "When I was your age I used to adore his books, because they were always about faraway places, and the servants always called their masters *bwana* and *memsahib*. They made me want to travel, even then."

A few minutes later the young man who was running the launch reached out to take Mrs. Gardiner's hand and help her aboard. "Step right here, *memsahib*," he said.

Kim could scarcely believe her ears. She caught her grandmother's eye and winked solemnly. "Right out of the pages of Rider Haggard," she murmured as soon as she got a chance.

Not only the islanders' speech smacked of a novel from the last century. The Peponi Hotel also had a storybook quality about it. White-washed and sun-drenched, the steps of its long verandah were lapped by the high tide. Branches of casuarina trees waved in a light breeze, but the atmosphere was heavy and humid. Grandy claimed that she felt exactly like Sadie Thompson as she allowed the strongest of the boys to carry her ashore.

The Peponi, run by a Scandinavian couple, proved to be clean and comfortable, and even boasted electric lights installed the year before. Kim and her grandmother had a cottage to themselves, and before lunch took time for a swim, finding the water almost as warm as the air.

A few yards off shore drifted *horis*, small fishing boats manned by Bajun fishermen, who appeared occasionally on the hotel steps to sell the kingfish and young sharks they had caught. Larger, motor-driven boats also plied along the shore from the hotel to the town, four miles away, picking up or returning Peponi guests.

These numbered only eleven, among them a young couple who introduced themselves as Donald and Olive Cross. They occupied the next cottage, and invited the newcomers for a lemonade before lunch. Working under a grant from Oxford to study sociological conditions on Lamu, they were full of information about the island and its people.

Kim quickly decided that Donald Cross talked like a textbook, but he interested her nevertheless. He called the citizenry unregenerate, grasping, polite, and profoundly suspicious. "They're so cut off from the world that they're a law unto themselves," his serious, young wife added. "For eighteen hundred years they've been exporting ivory and rhino horn along with tortoise shell, and coconut oil, and no-body's going to make them stop."

"Do you think there's much smuggling—today?" Mrs. Gardiner asked.

Donald Cross said, "Of course, but by small boat only. At low tide the harbor entrance is only seventeen feet deep."

"I'm dying to see the town," Kim confessed. "Do you think we could go in after lunch, Grandy?"

"Ride in with us," Olive Cross suggested. "We have a boat coming to pick us up at four o'clock."

As in most tropical towns, everything in Lamu was closed up tight during the heat of the day, the merchants doing business only in the early morning and late afternoon. When Kim and her grandmother stepped onto the main street from the dock, however, people were stirring once more and the shop shutters were open.

Close at hand the ancient city was far from glamorous. The streets were dirty, the plaster facades crumbling, and the people looked apathetic, as though they had neither the energy nor ability to do a good day's work.

"For tourists there's only one really interesting street," Olive Cross told Kim and her grandmother. "It runs parallel to the waterfront, right behind this row of buildings." She waved a hand and hurried off to join her husband, who was meeting a farm bureau official to talk about cows. "Have fun," she called back over her shoulder, "and take a good look at the carved doors, particularly at number 19."

"Number 19?" Kim stopped dead in her tracks. "Grandy, you don't suppose. . . ."

Mrs. Gardiner burst out laughing. "Probably mere coincidence," she said. "Still, anything's possible, and it's always interesting to have a focus for a sightseeing jaunt." She tucked a hand under Kim's elbow companionably. "Come on, sweetie. Don't just stand there. Let's go."

After the blazing sun on the waterfront, the narrow street seemed very dark indeed. High buildings rose on either side, nudging one another across a space no wider than an alley. Small, dusty shops occupied the ground floors in houses that might once have been handsome but were now virtual wrecks, their wooden doors hanging on rusty hinges, their balconies sagging, neglect eroding the plaster under the peeling paint.

"Goodness, it's positively creepy!" Grandy murmured. "I had no idea the place would be so run-down."

"It looks as if nobody's lifted a hand here since they freed the slaves," Kim said with a chuckle. "Not even to put up a number on any of the houses. Have you noticed that?"

"I hadn't, but you're quite right." Mrs. Gardiner stepped aside to let a man in a soiled white *jellaba* saunter by. "Of course, even if there *were* numbers, I suppose they'd be in Arabic."

Actually, several languages could be heard in Lamu: Swahili, Arabic, Somali, and among the shopkeepers a smattering of English, usually limited to a few key words. At a tiny store with a counter opening directly on the street, Kim and her grandmother stopped to buy a length of Katanga cotton for ten shillings a yard, and there they found a young woman who had been to school in Mombasa. She was delighted to practice her English when Kim ventured a question.

"Can you tell us how to find number 19?"

The girl nodded quickly, her lips parting in a wide smile. "He very important man here. Everybody know Number 19." She glanced around, then lowered her voice. "You very smart."

Kim didn't feel smart. She felt puzzled, but her heart began to beat faster. "Can you tell me how to get there?" she asked.

"Sure, sure. Right on down this way. You see very fine, very tall doors."

There were many tall doors, but none of them—at least in Grandy's opinion—were very fine. Then, suddenly, number 19 materialized, a pair of high, magnificently carved, antique doors stained a rich black-brown. They were latched back on either side of an entrance to an antique shop, a likely destination for any visiting tourist. However, once over the threshold, the handsome carved doors seemed an illusion. Dust lay half an inch thick on a collection of sorry relics— worm-eaten images of saints, crippled chairs, crudely inlaid Moroccan chests, even an old chamber pot.

"Ugh!" Kim grunted descriptively.

"Sh!" her grandmother cautioned, although the shop seemed to be deserted. A ramshackle desk occupied one corner, but the chair behind it was empty. At the back of the store, however, was another carved door, which was closed.

After poking around for a few unprofitable minutes, Grandy went boldly toward the door, grasped the iron handle firmly, and gave a tentative shove. It opened at once, with surprising ease, onto an interior courtyard of such unexpected charm that she gasped. "Kim! Come look!"

Bougainvillea climbed an ancient pink stone wall, and a marble fountain was surrounded by a bed of flowers that gratefully drank the water from its overflow. There was an iron table with four chairs, and the tiled floor had been swept clean of fallen leaves. Instead of mouldering into decay like the rest of Lamu, this patio was astonishingly well kept.

"Is there something I may do for you ladies?"

The accented English was precise, the voice silky but somehow menacing. Kim whirled around to face a thin, slight man well past middle age, who was wearing a crocheted Berber hat and an immaculate *jellaba,* from under which yellow Moroccan slippers peeked. His face was the color of parchment, crisscrossed with fine lines, and his eyes were black and shrewd. As Mrs. Gardiner turned, more composed than Kim, and faced him, there was no change in his expression to indicate whether he resented such trespassing or was merely amused.

"We were looking for number 19," she said.

The Arab, whom Kim privately nicknamed Flannelfoot because his entrance had been so silent, made a slight bow. "I am at your service," he said.

So this was Number 19—a man, a legend perhaps in Lamu—not an address at all! Kim felt out of her depth. How could Grandy excuse their intrusion, or invent an errand? She stood twisting the strap of her purse and waiting anxiously for any explanation that might be forthcoming.

"You have a very beautiful garden," Grandy said smoothly, turning back to the courtyard. "I am a gardener myself, and I realize that water must be a great problem here."

"It is most certainly a problem, madam, but surely that is not why you have come, to discuss gardening. Someone has sent you, perhaps, to inquire about Arab chests?"

"No," Grandy said. "No, not chests. Frankly, I was hoping that some leopard skins might be available."

Almost imperceptibly, Mrs. Gardiner had moved forward from the door until she was well inside the courtyard. Kim stayed close to her, and the Arab slipped over the smooth tiles as silently as a wraith and closed the door with a murmur of apology. "If I may." Then he added, "The dust from the street. . . ."

187

Mrs. Gardiner nodded, seeming quite unalarmed, but Kim felt as though she had walked knowingly into a lion's den. She didn't like the look in Flannelfoot's eyes.

"Won't you sit down?" The Arab's tone was polite, but Kim felt sure he was appraising the square-cut diamond in her grandmother's ring as he pulled back a chair.

Grandy played the rich American to perfection. She perched on the edge of the seat, keeping her back straight and her pocketbook placed conspicuously on her knees, while Kim put the clumsily wrapped parcel of cotton dress goods on the table and started to retie the skimpy string. Anything to keep her eyes from meeting Grandy's! This was a game that one must play alone.

"Leopard skins," said the Arab after an interval, "have become very scarce, and therefore very valuable."

"So I understand." His remark didn't seem to faze Grandy one bit.

"May I ask how you heard of me?"

That does it, Kim thought as she fiddled with the string nervously. She'll never be able to dream up an answer. Good grief!

However, she had underestimated the measure of her grandmother's poise. "From an Indian export shop in Nairobi," Mrs. Gardiner replied smoothly, and opened her pocketbook. "I forget the proprietor's name, but I have his card somewhere, I'm sure."

"No matter."

Mrs. Gardiner raised innocent eyes to the Arab's face, while Kim became more confused than ever. What key had Grandy turned that made him feel secure?

"You understand," the Arab said without further palaver, "that any transaction must be in cash."

"Will American dollars be acceptable?"

To this question there was no possible answer but "Of course."

Kim stepped back, clutching her parcel like a lifeline. Grandy was gambling at a table where the stakes might be uncomfortably high. Furthermore, neither of them carried much cash, only travelers' checks.

Flannelfoot, however, was apparently convinced that his potential customer came with good credentials. "There are some skins you may be interested in at my go-down," he said, then glanced at Mrs. Gardiner's feet. "It's not a very long walk."

"What is a go-down?" asked Kim, trying to sound curious rather than suspicious.

"A warehouse, a storage place," Flannelfoot explained, deadpan.

"Oh, I see."

The remark was an overstatement. Kim did not see at all. She didn't see what her grandmother was up to, nor did she understand why the Arab's attitude suddenly had changed. Almost unctuously, he led the Americans through the dusty shop and along a series of narrow side streets, until finally they reached a nondescript, windowless building with a padlocked door.

"One moment, please." From the folds of his *jellaba* Flannelfoot pulled out a bunch of keys and without difficulty found the one he sought. As he bent to fit it into the lock, Kim caught her grandmother's eye and tried to indicate that she disapproved of this expedition by solemnly shaking her head.

Grandy merely raised her eyebrows and smiled faintly—a pussycat smile, Kim thought in despair. Stepping across the threshold into a lofty storage room, the little woman looked as innocent and as vulnerable as a kitten.

The place was dim and dry and dusty, with the ubiquitous dust of Kenya that had drifted down even here to the edge of the Indian Ocean. Several pairs of Lamu's carved doors stood leaning against a wall, and some lengths of wrought-iron balustrade, relics of the days when wealthy Arabs had estates near this decaying city, lay rusting on the floor.

The antique dealer clicked a switch, and overhead two naked bulbs glowed faintly. There was a sound of scurrying—rats? Kim wondered with a shudder—and of an unmuffled yawn as a black figure disengaged itself from a stack of burlap sacks. "My watchman does not seem to have been watching," the Arab said to Mrs. Gardiner with a humorless smile.

There followed a series of brief, staccato orders, resulting in a good deal of heaving and tugging on the watchman's part. From under the burlap sacks he unearthed a huge, nail-studded Arab chest, fastened with a shiny new padlock. For this Flannelfoot also had the proper key.

When the chest was opened, Kim stifled a gasp. It was filled with tawny leopard skins, of which there must have been a dozen or more. At his employer's instruction the watchman took them out, one at a time, and spread them across the mound of burlap bags like a silken carpet, while Mrs. Gardiner examined each one carefully.

Even an inexperienced eye could see that the quality was superior, but Kim's grandmother was hard to please. "They're very nice," she said, "especially this one. You see, I much prefer the smaller spots. Now, if you could find two others, perfectly matched—" She broke off and spread her hands appealingly.

The Arab looked indignant. "You are asking the impossible, madam."

"Surely not the impossible," said Mrs. Gardiner gently. "It will be difficult, certainly, but I am prepared to wait, if necessary—and to pay."

"You are aware of the cost of a single skin of this quality?"

Mrs. Gardiner nodded. "Quite."

Kim could tell that the Arab was uncertain what his next move should be. He wanted to press the sale of the skins on hand, but he envisioned a handsome bonus if this rich client's every demand could be met.

In a calculated aside to her granddaughter, Mrs.

Gardiner said, "I once saw Mrs. Kennedy's coat, and I've always wanted one just as fine." Kim nodded, hoping the Arab didn't know that leopard coats were now considered, among her grandmother's friends, socially unacceptable.

Flannelfoot, evidently having considered the odds, spread his hands, prepared to accept present defeat in the hope of a later victory. "There are bound to be many problems," he said. "The finding of a ship, of a courier—"

"Of course. I am prepared to meet the extra expense." Mrs. Gardiner smiled encouragingly.

"Then perhaps you will be willing to give me something on account," suggested the Arab with courtesy. "Say a thousand dollars, which will be less than the cost of this single skin."

Kim swallowed hard. Grandy had escaped several traps, but there always seemed to be another set and ready. However, faced by this clever snare, Mrs. Gardiner simply burst out laughing. "I'm afraid American ladies do not carry such large sums on their persons. It will be better for me to deal through your man in Nairobi, or in Mombasa, if you prefer." As she spoke she was moving slowly but steadily toward the go-down's street door. She seemed in no special hurry, but Kim realized that Grandy was as eager as she to get safely outside once more.

"Why should I prefer Mombasa?" the Arab asked, a note of suspicion creeping into his voice.

"Well, you see we only touch down at the airport in

Nairobi, while in Mombasa I'll have time to get some travelers' checks cashed."

Greed was Flannelfoot's undoing, greed and his inability to conceive of a woman of Mrs. Gardiner's demeanor as either quick-thinking or devious. Keeping close to her side, opening the door and holding it, the Arab admitted having a representative in Mombasa and asked if she had a calling card on which he could write the necessary address.

"Of course." Kim's grandmother stepped outside quickly and found a card in her purse. "Here you are."

"Thank you." The Arab carefully wrote on the back of the small card, then returned it to his prospective customer, again letting his eyes rest on her beautiful diamond ring.

Standing at her grandmother's shoulder, Kim read the message Flannelfoot had written: "Ahmed—Ind. Ex." Following it was a name with an address on Kilindini Road.

"Index!" Kim gasped before she could control herself.

At once the Arab's eyes narrowed. "What did you say?"

"N—nothing," Kim blurted. "I was just wondering what Ind. Ex. stood for."

"Indian Export, of course, dear," said her grandmother indulgently.

Tucking the informative card back into her pocketbook, she shook hands with the Arab politely and walked away.

193

14

Once alone with Kim, Grandy's elation knew no bounds. "We did it!" she crowed. "We got what we were after. At last we know what Ind. Ex. stands for and we have an actual name and address. With our help John Sanderson may break the combination yet!"

"You did it, you mean. I never saw such a cool customer!" Kim was full of admiration for her grandmother's tour de force.

Riding back to the Peponi in the bow of a native boat, hired casually at the Lamu dock, each wished that it were tomorrow morning, rather than on the day after, that they would be heading back to Mombasa. They consulted together and agreed that they wouldn't budge from the Peponi's beach tomorrow. To tempt fate again would not be wise.

The following morning, lying in long chairs on the

verandah of their cottage, both Kim and her grandmother wrote accounts of their discovery in Lamu.
Kim's would go to John Sanderson, Grandy's to Bill
Parson in the Serengeti. This duplication would be
a safeguard, in case one note went astray.

Kim didn't share her grandmother's feeling that
their adventure was thus concluded. She yearned for
Neil to be in on the finale, since he had been beside
her in the first act. Common sense told her that the
show was over, but Kim was young and eager. If only
they were going back to Nairobi. . . . If only Mr.
Sanderson had received her note and would miracu-
lously appear in Mombasa. If, if, if. . . .

On the morning of the scheduled departure from
Lamu, tea arrived, as usual, at dawn. The luggage
was ready and the launch waiting by eight o'clock. The
return trek through the mangrove swamp was completed with a minimum of mosquito bites.

"So far, so good," said Grandy, "but I'll feel easier
when I see that plane."

Not five minutes later the small, red Cessna alighted
like a bright dragonfly on the pig pasture, while the
chattering porters started across the field with the
bags. They were accompanied by a newcomer, a ragged
youth who had appeared out of the blue only a few
minutes before. Kim saw him hand the pilot a Manila
envelope and heard him ask if it might be delivered
to the desk clerk at the Oceanic Hotel.

This request was not unusual. Since there was no

telephone in Lamu, the charter pilots were errand boys of sorts. They brought fresh produce to the Peponi and took out mail and packages to be delivered in Mombasa quite as a matter of course.

The flight was fast and smooth, the landing easy. "I suppose you're staying at the Oceanic," the pilot said to Kim. "Could I trouble you to take this envelope to the desk clerk?"

Kim assured him that it would be no trouble at all and thanked him for a pleasant flight. Then she and her grandmother took a taxi to the hotel.

Unpressurized planes did not agree with Mrs. Gardiner, and she had acquired a headache, so she went up to the room at once, while Kim lingered downstairs to have a lemonade. When she opened her pocketbook to pay for the drink, she remembered her promise to give the desk clerk the envelope, and she walked back to the lobby to remedy her oversight.

A gentleman was registering at the moment, and although his back was toward her, Kim recognized the tall, military figure of Herr Otto von Starck. To see him in Mombasa was unexpected but not especially surprising. On this trip, Kim had long since learned, acquaintances were continually turning up.

She spoke to him pleasantly, and he bowed over her hand with his usual courtly manner, although he seemed to find it difficult to recall where they had met. "At the Parsons', in the Serengeti. But of course it was Grandy you talked to, mostly—Mrs. Gardiner. She's resting upstairs, trying to cure a headache."

After she had delivered the Manila envelope, and had handed over the letters to John Sanderson and Bill Parson to be stamped and posted, Kim remembered to ask the second clerk on duty if any mail had arrived, either for her or for her grandmother. "I'm expecting a letter from Nairobi," she said, "a very important letter. Can you look out for it, please?"

About to turn away, she realized that the head clerk had torn open the Manila envelope from Lamu and extracted an inner one, which he placed on the counter in front of Herr von Starck. "This happens to be for you, sir, I believe."

Kim loitered unashamedly. Who, on that wretched little island, could be communicating with the handsome German? It seemed so improbable that she was ready to ask him a direct question, but at that moment he slipped the envelope quickly into his pocket and turned away, to follow a bellhop toward the elevator.

"Guess who!" Hands covered Kim's eyes, until she broke loose and whirled around to look up into Neil's laughing face. She was so surprised that she threw her arms around his neck and hugged him rapturously. "I can't believe it! Where did you come from?"

"The Land Rover broke an axle a mile from the airport, and we've been stuck here, trying to get a new one from Nairobi, ever since. Peter's over at the garage right now, trying to speed things up."

"Oh, Neil, I couldn't be happier to see you!" Kim bubbled, then burst out with the question uppermost in her mind. "Have you reached John Sanderson?"

Neil shook his head sorrowfully. "I phoned half a dozen times, then finally discovered his line's out of order. In Nairobi that's par for the course."

Kim bit her lip in disappointment, but hurried on to her own news. "I've got a progress report, anyway. Wait till you hear!" She led him back to the corner of the salon where her lemonade was half finished and quickly brought him up-to-date on recent developments. "We know a good deal more than we did before," she concluded. "Besides being pretty sure that *Mahdi* is that coastal dhow, we know that Lamu 19 is a man and that Ind. Ex. stands for Indian Export. We even have the address of the branch in Mombasa." Kim rummaged in her purse. "See, I've written it down."

"Let's go have a look around," Neil proposed as Kim sucked up the last of the lemonade through a limp straw. "Index won't know us from Adam, and we might get a clue as to whether Mombasa 27 is today or whether it's another odd number like 19, with no relation to the calendar."

Kim, more than willing, picked up her purse and her big, straw sun hat. "But I'd better leave a note for Grandy telling her why you're here and where I've gone. She's resting, so I won't disturb her. I'll just slip it under the door."

In chipped gilt script the pretentious title *Indian Export Company* decorated the glass window of a nondescript store similar to a dozen others on Kilindini Road. Its one distinction lay in its location near the giant, metal elephant tusks, painted a convincing ivory color, which arched over the street to form a Mombasa landmark no visitor could miss.

Kim and Neil strolled past the place, entered a nearby shop to price some tourist trinkets, then returned and paused in front of the window. Affecting a casual interest in a piece of primitive sculpture displayed on a table, they decided to go inside.

A slender Indian girl, her lank dark hair caught back in a barrette, nodded to them indifferently from behind a glass case of gold jewelry. She was busy talking to a brawny young man in a T-shirt with an anchor tattooed on his arm, and could find time to be only barely civil to the two foreigners.

Kim picked up the piece of sculpture that had attracted her attention. She examined it critically, then carried it over to the girl. "Can you tell me anything about this?"

"It's Makonde, made in Portuguese East Africa."

"I see. Is the wood ebony?"

"Ebony?" Apparently the word was strange to the Indian. "I don't know," she admitted. "My father would know, but he isn't here just now."

"Will he be in later?" Kim inquired, still professing interest.

The girl turned to her companion, and appeared to repeat the question in an Indian tongue. In answer the young man shook his head, and the girl asked Kim, "Can you come back tomorrow? He'll be here then."

"No, I'm afraid not. We're in Mombasa only for today." Kim left the store reluctantly, feeling that she had learned nothing, but Neil caught her hand and hurried her along the street until they came to a taxi stand.

"That fellow looked like a sailor," he said as he opened the door of the lead cab. "Let's go have a look at the harbor and see if the *Mahdi* is still anchored there."

On the way through town Kim twisted her hair on top of her head and fastened it with a couple of pins, cramming the broadbrimmed sun hat down so that no casual observer could tell she was a redhead. She put on dark glasses, as did Neil. There was no telling whom they might encounter on the waterfront, and they both felt the need for at least a partial disguise.

The driver let them off at the end of a long wooden pier heavy with cargo. Bunches of bananas, stacks of Makura roofing, mangrove poles, sisal, great sacks of coffee beans, and big drums marked "Pineapple Juice" were ranged in orderly fashion along one side of the platform, while on the other side two dhows, firmly tied up fore and aft, floated quietly.

Several tourists, also equipped with dark glasses, were taking pictures of the boats, which were being loaded by a handful of sweating black laborers. "These aren't regular stevedores," Neil said to Kim as they started along the dock to mingle with the camera buffs. "Over here in the Old Harbor it's catch-as-catch-can. The organized stevedores work the big port."

Kim was paying no attention. "Look!" she whispered. "The second boat *is* the *Mahdi.*" She stepped along a little faster until Neil grabbed her arm.

"Don't act too interested," he warned.

Kim slowed her walk to a saunter and let her eyes roam over the cargo. How much of it, she wondered, is contraband? Somewhere along here, camouflaged and safe from prying eyes, are there leopard skins waiting—the very leopard skins brought down the Galana River by dugout? It was only too probable that this was their destination, that it was on the *Mahdi* the poachers hoped to spirit their goods abroad.

"Are there customs inspectors here, Neil?"

"Of course." Neil pointed to a couple of men in uniform moving among the bales and boxes midway down the wharf. "They pick up a lot of loot for the Ivory Room every month, but they can't open every last sack of coffee or bale of sisal. It would be an impossible job."

"Suppose," Kim said slowly, "that we should go to the customs office and tell the people there what we know. About the skinned leopard at Amboseli and the hides we saw in the Masai *manyatta* and in the dugout, about the slip of paper I found in the Volkswagon bus and Number 19's go-down on Lamu. Certainly then they'd believe the *Mahdi* ties in—it's right down there on paper—and so is Indian Export, for that matter. The customs men might call in the police and really rip things apart!"

"Or," suggested Neil, "they might treat us like a pair of hysterical kids."

"Oh, don't be so negative," Kim scolded. "If only John Sanderson were here!"

"Well, your note should have reached him two days ago," said Neil irritably, "but I don't see him riding up on any white charger. Maybe even your precious Mr. Sanderson thinks you're getting a little hysterical."

Kim was glad her sunglasses concealed the amusement that leaped to her eyes. She was glad Neil could still be jealous; he hadn't put her out of his mind the minute the plane to Lamu had taken off.

"Stand back, please, miss." An Indian in a dark Western suit, looking hot and uncomfortable on this humid morning, was clearing a path for still another lot of pineapple juice drums being trundled along toward the far end of the pier. Neil and Kim both forgot their spat in a resurgence of curiosity. Could this be the Index man?

He walked along behind the handcarts as though he had a job to do. Three of the camera enthusiasts followed him, because some small boys had begged to dive for coins at the end of the dock. Kim and Neil trailed along behind and helped supply change for the venture, inconspicuously keeping an eye on the Indian, who had opened a notebook and seemed to be checking a list.

Between the end of the pier where the boys were diving and the last of the big pineapple juice drums the distance was perhaps twenty yards. The outer pilings had sunk a little and the board flooring had a downward slope, which meant the tins had to be stood on end, a job that one man could barely manage alone. Kim stood watching the laborers at work, while at the same time she tried to invent a way to approach the Indian. The heavy drums rocked the loosely laid boards, and their contents gurgled as they settled into place. Meanwhile the Indian waited, pencil poised. Only occasionally did he make a check mark on his list. Most of the time he mopped his face with his handkerchief and seemed to be aware only of his own discomfort.

Kim walked out to the end of the pier, stood by Neil for a few minutes, then walked back again, aware that something was not quite right about the scene. As she strolled past the big drums again, she paused, as though in idle curiosity, and once more watched a stevedore rock a barrel into place. Curiously enough, this one seemed lighter than the previous ones, and was stained on top by a blob of bright green paint.

Kim glanced from the drum to the Indian, who was making a mark in his notebook, quite oblivious to the scrutiny of a young American girl. The next two drums had to be wrestled upright, and he ignored them, but the third was light enough for a man to hoist without any trouble. Again Kim noticed a green paint smear, on the side of the barrel this time, but very much in evidence.

Her heart beating like a trip-hammer, Kim went out to rejoin Neil. "I've got it!" she said. "I'm sure I know how the leopard hides are being shipped."

"How?"

"In those pineapple juice drums!"

"Oh, come!"

"I mean it," Kim insisted. "Come see for yourself. Watch the Indian, and watch the barrels marked with green paint. They're lighter than the others, and each time one appears he checks it off on his list."

"If that's true, we're in a dangerous spot," Neil said as he fell into step beside her. His eyes lifted to scan the length of the pier. "If we should be recognized—"

He had no sooner spoken than he ducked his head and drew Kim close to his side, as though he was intent on romance even at midmorning. "Good grief, Kim, there's that Masai with the gold tooth. See! Pushing the lead dolly."

Kim glanced briefly at the sweating stevedore, then on beyond him at a tall man striding along the pier with a familiar military gait. Herr von Starck had changed into lightweight khakis and donned a planter's rakish straw hat, but he was as commanding a figure as ever.

"Neil! That's a man I know—a friend of Grandy's! He'll help us."

She was about to start forward, ready to accost the German and pour out the story of her discovery, when Neil caught her elbow in a viselike grip and cautioned, "Wait!" He took her by the shoulders and turned her toward him, and Kim thought for a minute he was going to kiss her, right there in broad daylight.

She put both hands against his chest and pushed, a gesture that, from a distance, might have looked playful to an interested bystander. "Keep on acting," Neil murmured. "Pretend we're oblivious to the rest of the world. We're having a lovers' quarrel."

"Are you out of your mind?"

"Shut up," said Neil pleasantly, turning so that Kim's back was to Herr von Starck, although he could still keep an eye on the German. "For Pete's sake, Kim, can't you just *pretend* to like me?"

"I do like you, a lot. You know that, Neil! What's happening?"

"Your friend is heading straight for the little Indian. Now he's talking to him. The Indian is bowing and scraping as though he's taking orders from a big shot, a very big shot indeed. Kim, how well do you know this von Starck? Where did you meet him? Talk fast."

"At the Parsons', that night in the Serengeti. He quite captivated Grandy. She thought he was wonderful. Before that I'd seen him at Treetops, chatting with Willard—Vernon W. Bixel. Then this morning Herr von Starck checked into the hotel while I was at the desk." She gave a quick gasp. "Oh, Neil, I almost forgot. I brought a letter addressed to him from someone on Lamu."

Neil looked very sober, but at the same time excited. He drew Kim closer and hugged her, then whispered, his mouth against her ear, "Do just as I say. We've got to get off this pier without von Starck recognizing you. We've got a story now the police are bound to believe!"

The trio of tourists, having run out of both coins and film, were strolling back along the wharf, politely ignoring the romantic pair clinging to one another. Kim and Neil waited until they had passed, then fell in behind them, by unspoken consent allowing the strangers to run interference. The pier was long, but at intervals there was a good deal of activity, and with luck they wouldn't be noticed.

Heads lowered, arms around one another, they whispered together. "Don't look now," Kim cautioned, "but here comes the scar-faced bus driver, the one who had the code in his glove compartment."

Neil muttered uncomfortably, "The gathering of the clan."

"I doubt if he'll recognize me," Kim said optimistically. "He has no reason to remember that afternoon when he found me looking for Mopsy's gloves." She took a long breath. "Come on. It's now or never. We've got to get past von Starck!"

It was difficult to maintain a pretense of being relaxed, difficult to keep from breaking into a run, but Kim counted on her concealing hat and on the fact that Neil had never before encountered the big German. Besides, in the world in which Herr von Starck moved, young people in general were beneath his notice, which should give them a measure of security.

Kim couldn't, however, avoid a split second of sheer mischance. A vagrant breeze caught the brim of her light straw hat and suddenly lifted it off her head like a kite, while her hair, insecurely pinned, tumbled down in a copper cascade.

The hat went skittering seaward down the pier, and Neil reacted automatically, racing off after it while Kim stood not ten yards from the *Mahdi*, feeling like a Halloween prankster whose disguise has been ripped away.

A stevedore, trundling an empty handcart back toward shore, stopped to turn and grin. The Indian flicked an eye in the direction of the American girl, then returned to his business. Herr von Starck, however, glanced quickly from the flying hat to Kim's bright hair. There was no doubt that he recognized her, because his eyes became cold as ice.

He neither spoke nor moved, as Neil, at the far end of the dock, abandoned the hopeless chase and let the hat sail out to sea. Kim also stood utterly still, like a butterfly pinned to a piece of cardboard. She knew, beyond a doubt, that von Starck was the top man in the poaching ring, and that he couldn't afford to let her escape. He obviously was aware that she knew too much, that in spite of her youth she was a serious threat. He would have to act—and act fast!

A fear beyond terror—beyond any emotion she had ever known—clutched at Kim's racing heart. On one side of her lay the *Mahdi,* where a net filled with the first batch of metal drums was swinging over the cargo hatch. On the other side stood the German, calculating his next move. Twenty yards away, hurrying back to her after his fruitless chase, came Neil.

As though she were caught in a nightmare, too frightened to scream, Kim stood frozen, knowing that von Starck could reach her long before Neil. Surrounded by his henchmen, the stevedores and crew of the *Mahdi,* he could do anything he chose. And at the moment the German leaped across the intervening drums and reached her, Kim could foresee her fate. She'd be thrown aboard the *Mahdi* with the rest of the cargo, stowed away and delivered to some remote port like any other piece of contraband.

Finally Kim moved. She turned and tried to run, but before she had taken a step, her body was pinned against the German's chest with a strong, uncompromising arm, and a hand was clapped over her mouth.

This can't be happening! Kim thought wildly. Right in broad daylight in front of a dozen onlookers, he can't kidnap me! Yet she realized that the tourists by now were back on shore, that the customs men, their job done, had retreated to their shed, and that the only people to see the incident were in von Starck's gang.

She kicked out wildly, banging her heels against the German's shins and thrashing about in his grasp. Her foot hit a metal drum, knocking it on its side, and she saw it go careering down the slope of the pier, picking up speed as it headed straight for Neil.

"Hey!" She heard his cry of alarm as Neil jumped aside and came racing toward her. Of course he'd never reach her! He was in as much danger as she.

And Grandy! What about Grandy? Anxiety made Kim fight with renewed strength. She bit savagely at the hand clapped over her mouth just as her captor reached the gangplank leading to the deck of the dhow.

She heard a muted splash, a burst of shouting, a piercing whistle. Then a heavy fist crashed into the side of Kim's head and she could feel herself falling, falling, spinning into a well of oblivion as black as night.

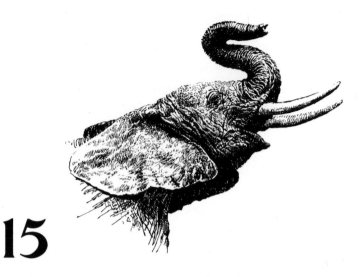

15

Kim struggled back to consciousness slowly, aware of a rocking motion and a pair of strong arms carrying her. The glare of the sun was hurting her eyelids. Her head ached, and her neck was stiff.

Then the sun, mercifully, was blotted out. She was being lowered to a hard surface—the floor, a bench? She put a hand to her forehead, then to the side of her cheek. Remembrance flooded back in a terrifying gush and she struggled to sit up.

"Keep still, Kim. Lie quiet for a bit. You'll be all right."

The voice was gentle and masculine, but it wasn't Neil's. Kim couldn't place it. She opened her eyes, feeling the lids flicker with the effort, and looked up into John Sanderson's concerned face.

"Neil . . ." she murmured. "Where's Neil?"

"He's all right, too. He'll be here in a minute."

Kim gave a sigh of relief and closed her eyes once more, hoping her head would stop pounding. A wave of nausea washed over her; then somebody held a paper cup of cold water to her lips. She sipped it gratefully and felt slightly better. "What happened?" she managed to ask.

"You fought like a vixen," John Sanderson said with a soft chuckle of admiration. "There was no choice for von Starck. He had to knock you out."

Kim touched her cheek again, ruefully. "He certainly did a good job of it." She stretched her jaw tentatively. It seemed to be working. "Do I still have all my teeth?" she asked.

"Every last one." It was Neil's voice speaking now. He was standing above her, smiling. Kim raised her hand so that he could hold it, then wearily smiled back.

Two strange men in uniform arrived to hover over her, and Kim began to feel foolish, stretched out this way. She took a firmer grip on Neil's hand and managed to sit up, still wishing the spinning in her head would quiet down.

She was inside a small building, which must be the customs shed, she reasoned. Men were hurrying to and fro, some in policemen's uniforms, some in the lightweight khakis of customs officers. There seemed to be a lot of controlled excitement in the air.

"Thanks to you, we got most of the gang, Kim,"

211

John Sanderson said, "along with a big haul of leopard skins. Most important of all, we caught von Starck red handed, and we've booked him for assault and battery, as well as for shipping contraband."

"He is the head of the poaching ring?" Kim murmured.

"We think so. The Indian Export man claims he's the top dog, and he should know."

"There's a man in Lamu," Kim said. "An Arab called Number 19. He could be pretty important, too." She took a long, tremulous breath. "Grandy will tell you all about him. Somebody ought to phone Grandy," she added. "She'll be worried about me."

"We've already tried," said John Sanderson. "She isn't in her room."

Forcing herself to concentrate, Kim said, "But she must be. Unless she's gone down to the pool for a swim."

"She isn't anywhere in the hotel," Neil said. "We had her paged. Peter's been waiting in the lobby for nearly an hour, and he says she hasn't gone out or come in."

Kim managed to get to her feet, and stood swaying. "We've got to get back there," she said shakily. "Something must be wrong!"

Crammed into the hotel elevator were Kim, Neil, Peter, John Sanderson, two policemen, and the assistant manager, who had come along more out of curiosity than from dedication to his job. The Oceanic rarely had any excitement to speak of, and he wanted to see why the little American woman who had registered just a few hours before should be the focus of so much attention. He carried a passkey that could be used, if necessary, to open the door.

Kim's ordinary room key proved to be quite adequate, however. Although her hand was trembling, the latch yielded readily, and a moment later the door swung open to reveal an astonishing sight.

Grandy was sitting in a straight-backed chair, her arms lashed behind its back, her ankles tied together with a belt from one of her dresses, a white linen towel fastened as a gag across her mouth. In spite of the fact that she was quite helpless, her eyes were sparkling with fury, and she was making a sound in her throat that sounded like an enraged cat.

"Mrs. Gardiner!" Peter was across the room in a flash, with Neil a close second.

The moment she could speak Grandy cried, "That horrible man! That wretched German! I've never been so humiliated in my life!"

"What happened?" Kim repeated the same question she had asked in the customs shed.

"I was just going out the door, on my way downstairs to buy some aspirin, when who should come along the hall but Herr von Starck. You remember him from the Parsons', Kim. He was perfectly charming, I thought then."

Kim couldn't resist grinning. "And now?"

"He's a roughneck!" Grandy said. "That's all he is. A roughneck disguised as a gentleman. Do you know what he called me? 'An interfering old woman.' Of course not at first. Not until he got me tied up and gagged. Then he accused me of lying to that Arab in Lamu. Now how could he have known about that?" Her eyes flicked to the two policemen and finally to John Sanderson. "Goodness," she said, "when did you get here? Are you going to catch that scoundrel? Is that why you've brought along the police?"

"You'll be relieved to know that von Starck is already in jail," John Sanderson said. "A lot has happened this morning, Mrs. Gardiner, and we'll tell you the whole story." He glanced around the disheveled room. "But don't you think a quiet corner of the lobby will be more comfortable?"

The entire group trooped back downstairs, and the assistant manager reluctantly returned to his office, while one of the policemen also excused himself. John Sanderson introduced the officer remaining as Constable Eboo, who wanted to make a full report on the events leading up to the apprehension of the poachers at the Old Harbor pier.

The capture of the other members of the gang was news to Mrs. Gardiner. "Wonderful!" she cried, as soon as she was apprised of the circumstances. Then she said regretfully, "But I seem to have missed all the fun."

"It wasn't such fun." Kim's swollen cheek was hurting and she sounded rueful. She gave her version of the happenings on the pier, and explained how she had detected that the drums marked "Pineapple Juice" were far from uniformly heavy. "How could the customs people miss discovering the same thing?" she asked.

"Apparently," John Sanderson replied, "they checked the shipment *before* the last batch of drums was delivered. The containers they tested were filled with liquid, and that's all they cared about."

"The one you kicked over with your foot was really the giveaway," Neil broke in. "It went rolling off the end of the dock, then floated in on the tide. While you were out cold, Kim, a chap in a rowboat hauled it ashore, and it was opened right under the eyes of Mr. de Souza himself."

"The Ivory Room will be piled high with loot!" Grandy cried.

"How did Mr. de Souza get into this?" Kim asked.

"He was alerted by me," John Sanderson said. "When I got your note I telephoned him and asked him to station police at the head of the pier where the *Mahdi* was being loaded. Then I hopped the first plane out of Nairobi this morning and came along as fast as I could."

"You certainly arrived in the nick of time," Neil muttered.

Kim could tell he was trying to sound grateful, although a residue of jealousy still remained in his tone. She smiled at him across the low table, where cold drinks had just been put down, then lifted her glass and raised it to him in a silent toast.

"The important thing," John Sanderson explained, "was to keep the raid a secret until the last possible minute. We wanted to catch as many of the poaching combine as possible. That's why I had to let you walk into a certain amount of danger," he added, speaking directly to Kim.

"You knew I was there all the time? Well, it does seem you could have come to my rescue five minutes earlier!"

"We couldn't possibly, not before von Starck made a move."

"You can't arrest a man on suspicion alone," Constable Eboo said. "Two things happened at the same time. The German tried to drag you aboard the dhow, and the drum went flying down the pier into the water. You see, the fact that it floated instead of sinking was our first clue to what it contained."

"Who else did you pick up?" asked Peter, leaning forward and addressing John Sanderson.

"A Masai from Ngorongoro, the one who helped ferry the skins downriver in a dugout, and a friend of his who was also in on the act. The Indian who worked for the combine in Mombasa under cover of Indian Export. A couple of sailors who are actually paid thugs. The captain of the *Mahdi*, who has been running contraband for years, if our suspicions are correct. A scar-faced character who claims to drive a safari bus, but who seems to know a little more than he should about the poaching racket."

"He could be the fellow Mopsy traveled with," Kim said in an aside to her grandmother, then told the policeman about the big wad of bills stashed away in the Volkswagon's glove compartment, and her subsequent discovery of the confusing words on the scrap of paper she had found.

"That paper, if only we had known it, was the clue to this whole operation," said Neil.

"I still don't understand," confessed Mrs. Gardiner, "quite how Number 19 fits in. The paper certainly proves he is part of the combine, but why should he be holding all those beautiful leopard skins in his godown instead of getting them to Mombasa in time to go aboard the *Mahdi* along with the rest?"

"That's something we'll know only when we bring him in and get him to talk," said John Sanderson. "The police have two men flying to Lamu right now, and with luck we'll have the answer tonight. I suspect the Arab somehow failed to make a Mombasa connection, so he was trying to drum up a little trade on the side."

"How stupid of me to have delivered the letter from Lamu that exposed Grandy to von Starck!" Kim exploded.

"You couldn't have known it was intended for von

Starck, not until you saw the desk clerk hand it over to him," Neil said. "Remember that it exposed you as well as your grandmother. If it weren't for that letter you wouldn't have a black eye!"

"A black eye?" Kim squealed. She got a mirror from her purse and inspected her face. "It is *not* black, only sort of lavender," she objected ruefully.

"Going back to the Arab on Lamu," said Grandy, "of course I realize that the reason he thought I was on the level was because I mentioned Indian Export in Nairobi. Frankly, it was just a name that popped into my head. I must have seen it somewhere, I guess."

"It's the store where I bought my belt," Kim said. "You probably saw the name on the shopping bag." Then she turned pensive. "That's the place where I first saw Willard. Do you think, Mr. Sanderson, there might be an American by the name of Vernon W. Bixel connected with all this?"

"It doesn't seem likely, but tell me about him, Kim."

"Well, that's quite an order, because he keeps turning up." Kim glanced toward the main hall. "As a matter of fact he was supposedly heading for Mombasa. I wouldn't be a bit surprised to see him walk in any minute. He's that type." She launched into a description of their various encounters, while Constable Eboo made notes that would help identify this new suspect. "His wife's supposed to be laid up in a Nairobi hospital while he treks around the country looking like a white hunter," Kim concluded. "It all seems very strange to me."

"There was another man you mentioned, that night we had dinner at the Parsons'," said John Sanderson. "A Yugoslav with a wart on his nose?" Kim asked. "That's right. You saw him duck out of a store in Nairobi just after I came in. Then he turned up again at the Masai *manyatta* in the crater, didn't he?"

Kim nodded, but before she could speak Constable Eboo said, "We have a line on a man answering that description. He works out of Nairobi. I'll get in touch with our chief and see that he's arrested along with the rest of the Indian Export staff. Chances are he's involved with the gang as a runner. Everything seems to point that way."

Mrs. Gardiner stood up. "May we leave any other small points to be cleared up later?" she asked. "I'd like to get an ice pack on Kim's poor face." She shook hands with the policeman politely, then turned to John Sanderson. "Since Peter has just told me that his car won't be ready until tomorrow morning, I've persuaded him—and Neil, of course—to dine with us one last time, here this evening. You'll join us, I hope?"

"I'll be delighted, and by then we may be able to write the final installment of this adventure. I should have news from both Nairobi and Lamu late this afternoon."

Kim put on her prettiest dress for dinner, but she felt far from attractive, although the swelling on her face had subsided, and a nap had restored her customary bounce. Doctoring the bruise with some of her

219

grandmother's liquid makeup, she kept wishing that Neil could carry away with him a different image. "I look perfectly terrible!" she complained.

"You look wonderful!" Grandy insisted. "Just like a young international spy after a brush with the enemy."

"Battered but unbowed?"

"Neil will think you're perfectly beautiful," Grandy added to Kim's embarrassment. "He couldn't take his eyes off you this morning, he was so proud."

"Oh, Grandy!"

"Oh, Grandy, my foot. You've made a conquest, child. It's probably not your first one, nor will it be your last—"

A knock on the door interrupted her. Outside stood a delivery boy with a florist's box in which two white Vanda orchids were nested in shredded tissue. "From John Sanderson, perhaps?" Grandy pulled a card from a small envelope and read, " 'To my own particular heroines.' From Neil! Why, the dear boy."

When they met downstairs John Sanderson and Peter remarked on the flowers immediately. Not to be outdone, they consulted together and ordered a bottle of champagne. Kim, sipping her first taste of the sparkling wine, wrinkled her nose, not quite sure she approved. "It tastes a little like very tart ginger ale without the ginger," she said.

During dinner John brought everyone up-to-date on the latest developments. Number 19 had been brought to Mombasa, along with two confederates, and was trying to repudiate any connection with von Starck. "Of course he doesn't know about Kim's incriminating slip of paper, which indicates he may be second in command."

"Operating out of Lamu?" Peter sounded skeptical.

"It could be the perfect place," John said. "Tucked away in such a remote spot, an Arab antique dealer normally would be quite safe from police investigation. Lamu has been a smugglers' port for centuries, and the small boats that ply up and down the coast are sailed by fellows who welcome any kind of money that comes easy. In other words, if the big operation strikes a snag, the little one still brings in a handsome profit for the firm."

"The thing I can't get over," said Mrs. Gardiner, "is how many outsiders are involved. An Arab, a German, a Yugoslav."

"What about the Yugoslav?" asked Kim. "Have you heard from Nairobi yet, Mr. Sanderson?"

"No, but I'm expecting a message here," John replied. While dessert was being served, a few minutes later, he was called to the phone in the lobby, and the rest of the party waited impatiently for his report.

They knew the instant he crossed the threshold of the dining room that the news was good. With a grin and a hand raised in a signal of victory, he hurried across to the table and slipped back into his chair.

"The Nairobi police picked up Kim's man with the

wart on his nose two hours ago," he said. "They locked him into a cell with a clutch of Indians who were all weeping and protesting their innocence. Apparently the Indians made him so mad he squealed on the entire gang, naming names and everything.

"According to this chap there are fourteen men involved, and he bore out our guess that von Starck and the Arab are in the A and B slots in the combine. There are six runners, fences in four or more cities under the cover of Indian-managed export firms, and a couple of receivers in foreign ports. With all this data we should be able to round up the few stragglers in a very short time."

"What about Willard?" Kim asked curiously. "Was he mentioned?"

John Sanderson shook his head. "No. There wasn't an American on the list."

"Nor an Englishman," mentioned Neil slyly.

"Which is purely a matter of chance," said Grandy amid the consequent laughter. "We have just as many rogues and scoundrels in the United States and Britain as anywhere else. It's just that they're interested in other things." She pushed back her chair. "Much as I hate to say good-night, I'm afraid the time has come."

With Peter Kent and John Sanderson on either side she walked out to the lobby, stopping in front of the elevators to wait for Kim, who lagged behind with Neil.

"I'm going to miss you," he said, glancing down as though he wanted to fix Kim's face in his memory.

"I'll miss you too." The words were banal, but Kim almost choked on them.

"Will you ever come back?"

"I hope so. I'd like to, but—"

"Don't say *but*. It's an ugly word." Neil tried, unsuccessfully, to grin.

Kim caught his hand and squeezed it briefly. "I'll try to come back," she promised, as they approached the group by the elevators. "You have my address. Please write to me!"

Then her attention was caught by a commotion out near the big glass doors leading to the automobile entrance. Two black policemen were propelling a thin, bald-headed man in a green-checked sports jacket toward the street. The fellow was protesting in a voice shrill with indignation, which carried clearly across the lobby.

"You can't do this to me!" he cried. "I'm an American citizen!"

"Good grief!" Kim exclaimed, standing on tiptoe for a better view. "That's Willard! Vernon W. Bixel. And he's innocent."

The scene was so indescribably funny that everyone burst out laughing. Kim, however, felt suddenly anxious to make amends to the man she had maligned. Now she saw him for the first time, not as a potential menace, but as Mrs. Collins must have seen him—a bald-headed, bumptious fellow who lost all his swagger when he was without his wife.

223

Impulsively, Kim took a couple of steps toward the doors, then turned back. "He's absolutely terrified of women," she said with a chuckle. "He'd be more afraid of me than the police. You know," she added in an aside to her grandmother, "for once Mopsy had things figured out absolutely right."

John Sanderson said, "I'd better rescue him," and was about to start off when Grandy caught his arm.

"Let them go," she advised with an envious sigh. "To be arrested in Mombasa, on the shores of the Indian Ocean! Think what a story he'll have to tell his grandchildren!"

This book   be

M.